The
Accidental
Courier

Robert Darke

ISBN-13: 978-1492871064
ISBN-10: 1492871060

DEDICATION

This book is dedicated to Diana
for never ceasing to believe in me, even
when, at times, I stopped believing in myself.

CHAPTER ONE

This was the second time Harry Rodgers' path had crossed mine. Last time he was alive and unpleasant; this time he was just unpleasant. In death, his staring eyes still managed a remarkable degree of malevolence. The bullet hole in the centre of his forehead appeared to be glaring too, like an accusatory third eye following me around as I trespassed in his kitchen. I felt indignant; wanted to tell him he needn't look at me that way, that it wasn't me who'd killed him. But any conversation with a corpse tended to be one-sided at the best of times. Blood was pooling on the floor from the exit wound in the back of his head and I just wanted to get out of there before I was sick.

The kitchen sink was full of dirty dishes and the place stank of stale curry, cordite and death. I stood rooted to the spot; this was the first dead body I'd seen and I felt numb.

Gabriel Winsome limped around the corpse taking care not to step in the blood. He unfolded a sheet of heavy-duty plastic and placed it on the floor.

"C'mon, Marty," he said, "don't just stand there gawping, grab his feet and 'elp me wrap 'im up."

I'd long ago given up trying to get him to call me

Martin. I hesitated, looking at the swollen scabby ankles, criss-crossed with angry blue veins. Maybe gout had been the cause of Rodgers' ill-tempered disposition. Even wearing latex gloves, I felt squeamish about touching his skin, so I grabbed a fistful of fabric from each leg of his pyjama trousers and tried to lift him. All I succeeded in doing was pulling them down and exposing his private parts.

"Bloody 'ell!" Winsome exclaimed. "If you're gonna have sex with 'im I'll wait outside if yer don't mind!"

"Very funny," I said.

In the end, we resorted to rolling him onto the plastic sheet rather than lifting him, and Winsome set about sealing our makeshift body bag with duct tape.

"Let's get this lump of lard in the back of the van, and then we'll 'ave to come back and clean up all this frikkin' mess." Winsome glanced disdainfully at the blood on the floor.

The heavy body was literally a dead weight, and as we shoved and dragged him out of the kitchen and across the hall carpet, I accidentally knocked the phone to the floor. The line hummed into the silence.

"For Christ sake, Marty, look where you're going, mate!"

"I'd never have agreed to this if you'd told me we were shifting a body!" I protested, picking up the phone.

"That's why I never told yer. I knew yer wouldn't like it, but there wasn't no one else available and it 'ad to be done tonight."

"I never signed up for this!"

"I never signed up for this..." Winsome mimicked. "Did yer really think that Leon's paying you all this money just to drive a van? It's blood money, mate, so get used to it and shift yer arse — we've already been 'ere way too long!"

I bit my lip and continued with the task in hand. It was hard to believe that just a couple of months ago I was an ordinary business advisor, making a living in a mundane, nine-to-five job in a bank sub-branch in the quiet Cardiff suburb of Roath. Now, in a disturbingly short space of time, I'd become someone who shifted bodies around in the middle of the night. Looking back, I could see how easily I'd got sucked into this mess, but I had no idea how I was going to get out of it... and stay alive.

CHAPTER TWO

My world started to disintegrate on an early summer's day that started like any other Monday at the bank. I'd grabbed my usual cappuccino-to-go from Beth's Café and was sipping it, waiting for my PC to boot up, when my desk phone rang.

It was the manager, Darren Pierce. "My office now!"

A well-built woman in a heavily patterned dress two sizes too small for her sat to the right of Pierce's desk. I'd never seen her before. She remained silent, but seemed to be assessing me through dark, piggy eyes.

Pierce didn't bother introducing her. "Take a seat, Blake," he said.

Something was up; I'd been hauled in front of the manager many times but never before been invited to sit. Instead of coming directly to the point, Pierce began uncharacteristically rambling about world recession, the banking crisis, austere times. His eyes darting everywhere but never quite meeting mine, until he used the phrase "...means we have to prune out the deadwood..." when, finally, he shot one of his famous 'Piercing' glances at me.

Right on cue, the still nameless woman said she was from HR and launched into a well-rehearsed spiel. "As you know, the bank issued a statement, previously agreed with your union, and in line with all statutory obligations, that, following branch closures, a redundancy programme was necessary."

She paused for breath.

I bristled at her saying 'your union' as I'd never belonged to a union – although it now occurred to me that maybe this hadn't been the wisest decision in my life.

She outlined the deal on the table and finished by saying, "I must stress this is Voluntary Redundancy we're offering and you're not obliged to accept it. However, it's also a one-off, time-bound offer and, should you decline to accept, we cannot guarantee that you will not be made compulsorily redundant at a later time, and at less favourable terms. You have until the end of this week to decide."

Part of me had tuned out as I already knew where this was leading: I was being bought off for expedience. My career with the bank was over, and much to my amazement, instead of resentment, a wonderful feeling of freedom engulfed me. This was the catalyst that finally crystallised a loathing of the job that I'd been burying deep inside for years.

Pierce was sharp like his name: sharp-dressed, sharp-nosed, sharp-tongued, and now proving to be as sharp as pruning shears. Throughout the HR woman's speech, he watched out of narrowed eyes and I could tell my smile unnerved him as if I just might know something he didn't.

I'd rarely taken a spontaneous decision in my life, but without glancing at the HR woman, I said to Pierce, "You can have my decision right now. I accept."

"Excellent!" he declared, recovering quickly from my unexpected reaction. Scarcely able to hide his glee he added, "We shall of course miss you ...err, Blake, and I'd like to thank you on behalf of the bank for your many years of loyal service."

Even the HR woman squirmed.

"You needn't work your notice," he said, niceties over. "We'll pay you in lieu so you can leave today. Just leave your staff pass and the keys to your company car on your way out."

Pierce lifted his phone receiver and began dialling.

I managed to keep my bravado up until I closed his office door behind me, then my feeling of elation evaporated. I lowered my eyes and made straight for the privacy of a toilet cubicle where I sat head in hands wondering how I was going to go back and face the rest of the office. Four years ago Pierce's predecessor, a lovely old-fashioned bank manager, had presented me with a gold watch for twenty-five years service and now they dared to call me 'deadwood'. I clenched my fists until the nails dug into my palms and fought down the urge to punch a hole in the toilet door. Gradually anger gave way to despair and disbelief. I emerged from the cubicle and checked the mirror. A fifty-one year old man, slightly overweight, with black rings beneath the eyes stared back at me. I jabbed a finger toward the glass and declared venomously, "You're deadwood, you bloody Neanderthal, deadwood! Do you hear?"

I swilled my face with cold water, re-straightened my tie, combed what was left of my greying hair, and mustered what dignity I could to go and say goodbye to my colleagues.

*

I spoke first to Patrick, whom I'd sat opposite for the past fifteen years. "Has he called anyone else in?"

Patrick shook his head.

"Just me then..."

Patrick looked embarrassed. "Sorry mate."

"Don't be, it isn't your fault."

I checked my calendar – there was only one appointment scheduled for the day. Although my loyalty to the bank had evaporated I still felt some towards my clients.

"Can you see this guy for me at two o'clock?" I asked Patrick. "His name's Leon Cooper, he's quite a tough cookie and won't take kindly to cancellations and whatever you do don't call him 'Leo'. He hates that."

Patrick checked his screen and said, "Sure, I can see him for you, no problem."

I was going to warn him about the wealthy Mr Leon Cooper, one of my most unpleasant clients, but changed my mind. What the hell, I thought; Cooper's volatile temper wasn't going to be my problem anymore ...I was later to be proved very wrong on that score.

"Thanks, you may as well take on all these too," I said, emailing over my full client list.

I gathered together my few personal belongings, including the photos of Katrina and Ella. The bank's hot-desk approach and general policies discouraged bringing much personal stuff into the workplace. There wasn't much else to collect from my car either. All my personal stuff fitted easily into a briefcase I normally only used to carry sandwiches.

The other staff received the news with a mix of pity, relief that it wasn't them, and survivor guilt. A few of the women complained tearfully that they hadn't even had a chance to start a collection, or sign a card. They insisted I come back at the end of the week for a leaving do. I said "Yes," to pacify them but knew I wouldn't be doing anything of the sort. I gave the newest recruit my office stapler like I was passing a relay baton. Then I left, quietly passing through the heavy security door and leaving the branch where I'd worked most of my adult life.

*

On the pavement the enormity of my situation hit me. It was only 10 o'clock and the unexpected emptiness of my day stretched menacingly ahead. Without the company car I'd have to either walk home or catch a bus. How was I going to break this to Katrina? She'd not be pleased, that was for sure! Somehow in her twisted logic she would blame me for this whole mess. She wasn't going to take kindly to cutting down on expenditure either. The thought of facing her made me dawdle even more slowly and I decided to have another cappuccino in Beth's Café.

It was fairly quiet for once.

"Back so soon!" Beth said, with the first genuine smile I'd seen that day. "Another regular cappuccino to go?"

"Make it a large to stay."

Beth's shapely eyebrows vanished beneath her dark curly fringe and she made an 'O' with her mouth.

"The bank's just made me redundant after nearly thirty years."

"Oh no, poor you – go and sit down, love, I'll bring it over." She waved her arm towards the tables as if to say sit anywhere.

A few minutes later she placed a bucket-sized mug in front of me, then slid into the seat opposite. "If they can just cast you aside like that, with all your experience, then they don't deserve you. You're well shot of them!"

"I hadn't seen it quite that way, but I suppose you're right."

"Of course I am," she agreed, "what will you do now?"

"I don't know yet. Anything going here?"

She laughed, but we both knew I was only half-joking.

"I barely make enough to cover my bills," she said, shrugging.

I let it go, embarrassed.

Beth got up to serve a new customer.

Warming my hands on the mug, I stared out of the window. A horn blared as a white van double parked. The van driver appeared oblivious to the angry protest as he hoisted a large cardboard box onto his shoulder for the florist next door. I caught myself wondering what it'd be like to drive a van all day instead of sitting behind a desk. What the hell was I going to do? Should I sign-on at the Job Centre?

I wasn't one of the wealthy bankers with huge bonuses

portrayed in the press. I had made a fair living but I was by no means rich nor did I have a big stash of savings. I was a Business Development Manager in a backwater branch and the only reason I was given a company car was for the ever-decreasing visits to client's premises: so I'd been expecting it to go soon anyway, but not take me with it. The chances of finding a similar job in the current climate were slim. Besides, I'd had enough of a lifetime of wearing a suit and sucking up to people like that rich bastard Leon Cooper.

I finished the cappuccino and ordered another but this time Beth had a queue forming and she stayed behind the counter. She told me quietly that I could have this one on the house but I wouldn't hear of it. I wasn't about to start accepting charity from friends.

I made the second cup last an hour and it was cold before I finished it. The cafe began filling for the lunchtime trade and I didn't want to hang around in case someone from the bank came in. Anyway, it was time to walk home and break the news to Katrina and then, after she eventually calmed down, maybe we'd have a sensible discussion about what to do next. Some hope!

CHAPTER THREE

The walk home took nearly twenty minutes and I spent most of that time rehearsing how to tell Katrina. My black work shoes pinched and I was already missing my company car. I wondered how much of the lump sum, which amounted to about ten month's salary, I could afford for another car.

The four-bedroomed detached house in Penylan that we'd purchased just a few years ago stood at the end of a cul-de-sac of similar properties all built in the 1990s. It had been a stretch for us, and as it dawned on me that my days of a subsidised mortgage and cheap loans were over, I wondered how much the new monthly payments would be. If I didn't find paid work quickly, we might have to consider selling.

It felt odd approaching home on foot; our bedroom curtains were drawn so maybe Katrina was taking a shower. Ella would be at her sixth form college studying hard to get the grades for a place she'd been offered at Exeter University. The costs of putting her through uni suddenly scared me.

When I entered the hall I heard the shower running so didn't bother to call out. I slung my jacket over the banister, dumped the briefcase on the floor then made my way up the stairs. I felt sticky after the walk home and wondered fleetingly if Katrina might let me join her in that shower. I loosened my tie and vowed to look for a job where I didn't ever have to wear one again.

Katrina lay naked on the bed.

"Bloody Hell!" she cried. "You're home early."

Hastily, she tugged the sheets all the way up to her demure little chin.

I held onto the doorframe to steady myself and fought the bile rising in my throat. Another man's clothes were slung over the chair, a pair of Calvin Klein boxer shorts lay discarded on the floor. Katrina's eyes were wide, her dyed-blonde hair tousled and her ruby lipstick was smudged unattractively around her mouth.

"Who's in the shower?" I demanded, not really wanting to know.

Before she could answer a man's voice called from the other side of the en-suite door. "Care to join me, Katty Baby?"

"You'd better come out here, Tim," Katrina kept her voice low, urgent, warning. "Martin's home early."

"Katty Baby?" I mouthed in disbelief.

The water stopped abruptly and I heard the familiar creak of the shower tray as a man stepped out of my bathroom, still dripping wet, a towel wrapped around his midriff.

"Hello Martin," he said, one hand clutching the towel to stop it riding down over his paunch, his bald patch clearly visible through his wet hair.

I wanted to punch my neighbour's face into a bloody pulp and it took all my self control not to do just that. I stayed where I was clutching the doorframe so hard it hurt.

"Get dressed, the pair of you. I'll be waiting downstairs," I snapped, my voice sounded strangely quiet, given how I felt like screaming at them.

I went down the stairs on shaky legs, grabbing the

banister for support, made it to the drinks cabinet and poured a large brandy. I drank it straight down, feeling the liquor burn inside, and immediately poured another.

I was on the third glass when they sheepishly entered the living room. I pointed at Tim. "You can piss off right now, you're not needed here."

"Let's try and keep this civilised, shall we?" Katrina said, looking at me.

"Do you want me to stay?" Tim asked Katrina.

She shook her head. "I'll text you later."

He opened the door, then turned to me and said, "I'm sorry you had to find out like this."

"Just fuck off!"

Tim hesitated and turned to Katrina, who nodded at him to go.

We both waited in silence until we heard the front door close.

"Did you have to show yourself up, talking to him like that?"

"How am I supposed to talk to the bloke I've just caught screwing my wife?"

"We can't talk about this if you're going to be aggressive."

"In twenty six years of marriage have I ever hit you?"

"No," she admitted.

"And I'm not about to start now, although Christ knows you deserve it."

Katrina looked at the ground like she was seeing the pattern in the carpet for the first time.

"How long has this been going on?" I asked, realising I sounded like a cliché in a bad movie and not caring.

"About eighteen months," she replied in an almost-whisper.

"Eighteen months!" I couldn't stop my voice rising. "You mean you were screwing him behind my back while we celebrated our twenty-fifth anniversary?"

"It wasn't like that."

"Oh really? What was it like then? I can't wait to hear this!"

Katrina just stared at me.

"Does his wife know?" I demanded.

"Obviously not. Let's try and keep Miriam out of this."

"Oh yeah, let's not destroy Miriam's feelings: like that's not going to bloody happen!"

I went back towards the drinks cabinet.

"Martin, please don't drink any more; I think you've had enough."

"I haven't even started yet!"

"If you pour another drink I'll leave right now."

I stubbornly replenished my glass then turned and met her gaze.

"You still here?" I asked.

Tears glistened in her eyes. She stormed out of the room, slamming the door behind her and clomping up the stairs. I heard the bedroom door slam.

Finally, my own anger erupted and I flung one of our best cut glasses, still full of brandy, at the wall. Then, crumpling into the chair, I felt my own tears welling, put my head in my hands and sobbed.

It took me a while but eventually I regained some control. It was nearly half past four and Ella might walk in at any moment. I didn't want to be there. How could I face my daughter with this? What could I possibly say to her? I phoned for a taxi, then went upstairs. The bedroom door was still shut and for a moment I hesitated, unsure whether or not to knock. Then I told myself not to be so ridiculous; after all this was still my house. Katrina was curled on the bed. Her eyes were red and puffy and already a small pile of paper tissues was building on the floor.

"Leave me alone," she said.

"You needn't worry on that score! I've no intention of staying."

I yanked the suitcase from the top of the wardrobe, pulling down a shower of dust with it that made me cough, and began angrily tossing in shirts, pants and socks. I retrieved my toothbrush from the bathroom where I found the floor still wet with lover-boy's damp footprints.

"Where will you go?" Katrina asked.

"I'll find somewhere; don't bloody concern yourself."

"What should I tell Ella?"

"How the hell should I know? You got us into this flipping mess. You think of something."

"We should tell her together – but she doesn't need an upset just before her exams."

My inclination was to tell Katrina she should've thought about that before shagging our neighbour but she was right; Ella deserved better.

"Tell her I've been called away on a training course, filling in for someone who is ill. I need some time away from you, Katrina, to get my head around this."

"Where will you be? When will we talk?"

"I don't know yet. If you need me urgently call my mobile."

A text message arrived from the taxi outside.

I took a long and hard look at my wife and an overwhelming sadness engulfed me. I turned away quickly, not wanting Katrina to see it in my face.

"How's your day been?" the cabbie asked.

CHAPTER FOUR

The second question the cabbie asked was, "Where to mate?"

Such a simple, obvious question but it flummoxed me. I felt as though life had just set me adrift. In one fell swoop I'd become jobless and homeless and bewildered and aimless, and I had no idea where to tell him. In the end I said, "Just head towards town, please."

He dropped me near Queen Street and I wandered past the shops in a daze. I saw a tramp lying on a cardboard sheet in a doorway and realised if I didn't want to end up sleeping rough I needed to find a bed for the night.

I ran through a mental checklist of our friends but the trouble was after being so long married they were just that - 'our' friends, not 'my' friends and I couldn't help wondering whose side they would be on, mine or Katrina's?

In the end, I rang Patrick from the bank. He was more of a colleague than a friend but we'd known each other a good few years. He seemed happy enough to offer me the use of an air bed in his spare room, apologising that it was all he had.

*

Later, in The North Star, we sat opposite one another straining to make conversation. Patrick told me what had happened in the aftermath of my leaving which didn't amount to much and took only a few minutes.

"How did the meeting go with Leon Cooper?" I asked, more to make conversation than out of any real interest.

"He cancelled at the last minute. I'm seeing him tomorrow now. Does he do that kind of thing often?"

"He's a bit unreliable but when he does turn up his money's good. So keep the right side of him."

The conversation hit another brick wall.

Patrick hadn't mentioned my 'domestic crisis' and I respected him for not asking. However, once our steaks arrived, I felt the need to open up but first checked that no one on any of the nearby tables could overhear.

Speaking quietly so he had to lean forwards to hear me, I said, "Actually, Patrick, my day has been even worse than you can imagine..."

I told him all that had happened and he gaped at me, open-mouthed in shock.

"But I thought you and Katrina were happy together," he said.

"So did I! To be honest, I don't know what's hit me yet; or what the hell happens next."

"W...Well you're welcome to stay at my place for as long as you need," Patrick said.

"It's at times like these you find out who your true friends are," I said, and looked quickly away to hide the tears welling in my eyes.

Patrick seemed happy to listen without offering unwanted advice. When we got back to the flat he offered to put on a DVD but I just wanted to retreat to my makeshift bed and think things through.

As I lay on the air bed my mobile rang – it was Katrina. I let voicemail kick in, then switched the phone off. She could wait until morning.

I didn't feel in the least bit sleepy. I think it was about

4am that I decided I would never work for anyone else again. I would use my redundancy money before Katrina could get her grabbing hands on it and set myself up as a self-employed businessman. All I had to decide now was what line of business.

*

Unfamiliar movements and sounds woke me and made me wonder where the hell I was until the unwelcome memories of yesterday's events flooded back. I could hear Patrick taking a shower. There was no clock so I felt for my phone. The battery was low, then I realised I'd left the damn charger at home. I dialled my voicemail and listened to Katrina's message. She was slurring her speech and drunkenly rambling about how sorry she was I had to find out that way. I deleted the message.

There was a knock on the door. "You decent in there?"

"Yes, come in."

Patrick opened the door and remained standing just outside. He was suited and booted and looked anxiously in at me.

"I have to go to work," he said, almost apologetically. "T...There are cereals in the cupboard, milk in the fridge, and help yourself to toast and coffee. I've left you my mobile number in case you can't find anything – leave a voicemail or text me if you need anything. There's a spare key to the flat on the counter top. I'll be back around five thirty this evening."

"Patrick, I really appreciate this mate. You're a star!"

"Like you said last night, that's what friends are for. I...I meant it when I said you're welcome to stay as long as you need." Patrick smiled generously and then closed the door.

A little later, I decided I'd have a coffee and breakfast roll in Beth's Café.

It was hot and busy and full of cooked-breakfast smells that were difficult to resist. No wonder there was a queue at the counter! Beth didn't have much time for me other than to exchange brief pleasantries. I found a seat by the window and took a sip of coffee. A van double-parked outside and a scruffy looking driver in a red baseball cap sauntered into the cafe and hailed Beth who immediately sent two of the girls from behind the counter to help him load boxes of food.

Beth brought my breakfast roll to the table. Things were quieter now and she seemed happy to stop and chat.

"How are you my lovely? Have you decided what you're going to do with the rest of your life?"

I had no answer for that. Nodding towards the van, I said, "I didn't realise you did outside catering."

"Oh we've been doing it for quite a while now. In fact, it's the fastest growing part of my business and makes nearly as much profit as the cafe."

"Enough to employ your own driver?"

Beth grinned at me. "Can't afford that yet," she said then, lowering her voice she added, "That scruffy mongrel is from a local courier firm."

She had to return to the counter. I hadn't liked to ask how much the courier firm charged but they must be making money or they wouldn't be doing it. An idea started forming in my mind. I could soon research how much local firms charged for deliveries. What if I bought a small van and became a freelance driver? After all, I knew plenty of local business owners, many of whom I'd helped to secure loans in more prosperous times. The idea of having no one to answer to but myself and the freedom of the open road appealed, but my years in the bank had taught me not to romanticise too much. I would have to investigate and see just how viable it might be. All the same, I felt excited by the prospect – it was the first positive thought I'd had in twenty-four hours.

My phone lit up and I heard the voice of Yoda from Star Wars telling me I had a message from the dark side. Yoda was right, it was a terse text from Katrina that read: *We need to talk.*

I realised, in all the traumas of yesterday, I still hadn't

told her about my redundancy so she'd have assumed I was at work and be puzzling why I'd come home so early. I knew we had to talk but still wasn't sure I was ready yet. But when would I ever be ready for the kind of conversation we must have? I texted back one word *When?*

A few minutes later Yoda spoke again: the message read *How about a meal at Deangelo's tonight about 8pm?*

So, she wanted to be somewhere public and neutral, presumably to avoid Ella overhearing anything. I texted back *OK please bring my phone charger and my iPod.*

It was still only ten-thirty in the morning.

I wandered aimlessly around the shops. There were several things I might have bought without a second thought if I were still employed but knowing I currently had no income was a powerful dissuader. Already I regretted saying I'd meet Katrina in a restaurant. I went to the library to look through papers for suitable vans. I was shocked: the price of some of the newer vans would make a significant dent in my redundancy money. There were a couple of older vans but they had very high mileages. Reliability would be key to any delivery business, so leasing might be a better option. All the same, I made a note of a couple of telephone numbers for sellers of the cheaper models.

I bought a packet of prawn sandwiches and a diet Coke and returned to Patrick's flat. A daytime TV programme I'd never seen before invited people to choose between accepting a dealer's offer for their bits of old junk, or selling them at auction. I drifted off to sleep without ever finding out what they decided to do.

That evening, Patrick returned from work with a huge Hawaiian pizza for us both to share. I didn't have the heart to tell him I was meeting Katrina for a meal, so I just quietly ate the pizza. Besides, I wasn't sure how much I'd feel like eating later anyway.

Deangelo's was buzzing with activity and the bar was crowded with folks waiting for their tables, or ordering takeaways. There was no sign of Katrina so I ordered a pint of lager and a martini. I was already halfway down the pint by the time she arrived. She seemed grateful I'd already bought her a drink and took a demure sip.

"How's Ella?" I asked, determined to keep things civilised.

"She's fine. She's gone to see a film with her friends and I had to run her into town. That's why I'm late, sorry."

"Does she suspect anything's up between us?"

"I don't think so. She seemed happy enough to believe you're away on a course."

An awkward silence developed and then we both spoke at once and immediately stopped.

"Let's choose a meal first, shall we?" I said, handing her a menu.

Katrina ordered lasagne. I looked for the cheapest menu option and ordered a salad. Katrina raised her eyebrows in surprise. "I'm not hungry," I said.

"Where did you go last night?" she asked.

"I had a threesome with two women I picked up in a bar. What's it to you?"

"Martin, please, let's be civilised about this. I didn't come here for a fight."

"I'm staying with Patrick," I said, trying to keep my voice even.

"Oh good, I didn't like to think of you staying all alone in some featureless hotel room."

"Did you remember to bring my phone charger and stuff?"

"Yes, I brought your electric shaver too," she said, "and there's another suitcase of fresh clothes and underwear in the boot of my car."

"Thanks," I said, rubbing the back of my hand across the stubble on my chin; until then I hadn't even realised I'd not shaved.

The waiter brought our meals and we ate the first few mouthfuls in silence.

The table was private so at least we could talk without fear of being overheard, so long as we didn't raise our voices.

Katrina began. "I'm truly sorry you had to find out about Tim and me in that way. I was planning to tell you soon."

"Must've been quite some plan, if it was 18 months in the making." I couldn't hide my bitterness.

"It started off as just a fling; it was only much later that it grew into something more serious."

"Just a fling! How can you be so casual about adultery?"

"Oh, come on Martin, it's not as if you're a complete innocent. What about that conference in Manchester?"

"I was drunk; it was a one night stand, not something I carried on for months behind your back!"

"And would you ever have told me, if I hadn't overheard you having phone sex with her a week later?"

"It was never going anywhere," I said.

"And I thought this wasn't going anywhere too. It just happened and then we swore we'd never see each other alone, or speak of it, again. And we didn't, not for ten months but then we realised neither of us could fight our feelings for each other any longer."

"For God's sake! Spare me the clichés!"

"Please Martin, I know how much this must be hurting you, but I was going to tell you I'm in love with Tim. I was just waiting until after Ella had finished her 'A' levels."

She reached across the table to rest her hand on mine but I snatched it away.

"However things work out between us, we have to put Ella's happiness first, Martin. You do agree with that, don't you?"

I nodded, unable to speak as I imagined all the time in the past eighteen months we'd been at neighbourhood gatherings with Tim and Miriam. And the odd occasions he and I had played golf while all the time he was 'at it' with my wife. I wanted to kill the bastard and could feel my cheeks burning.

Katrina kept her voice calm and slow. "The thing is, Martin, I'm going to ask you for a divorce but I want us to try and hang on and keep it from Ella for just another two weeks until her exams are over. Do you think you can do that? For Ella's sake?"

I screwed my eyes tightly closed fighting a wave of emotion. I felt her hand on mine and this time I didn't pull away from her touch. Slowly, as I regained my composure, she withdrew her hand.

"Martin," she said, tentatively, "one thing I have been wondering is how come you came home so early yesterday?"

"I was made redundant," I blurted, at last meeting her eyes and seeing genuine sorrow in them.

She came around to my side of the table, "You poor thing, oh my God," she said, and gave me a hug. I'd promised myself not to get angry, or upset, but suddenly it was all too much for me and I buried my face in her shoulder, fighting back the twisting in my guts. I was conscious that other diners were watching us. I felt pathetic.

CHAPTER FIVE

Patrick and I ate our breakfast together in near silence. I was shattered, having lain awake most of the night turning things over and over in my head.

"Is it OK if I stay until Friday?" I asked.

"Of course it is, I told you – stay as long as you need."

"Thanks, Patrick, you've been a good mate and I appreciate you putting up with me. I'll go back home on Saturday but only for a couple of weeks, until Ella's finished her exams and then we'll be separating and eventually divorcing."

"It really is over then?"

"I think so mate, she says she's in love with this Tim and that he's leaving his wife so they can be together." I let out a slow sigh; it was still hard to hear my own voice saying those words. "I don't know what he's got that I haven't – apart from slightly less hair on his head and a job."

Patrick looked guilty. "No one understands why Pierce singled you out for redundancy. They all feel bad about it, me too."

"Don't feel bad, I never really hit it off with that bastard and your target results for the past year have been way ahead of mine. Hell, if I'd had to choose who to keep between you and me I'd have picked you too!"

"What are you going to do with yourself today?" Patrick asked.

"I'm going to get around my contacts and sound them out about local courier services – I'm thinking of buying a van and going freelance."

"Sounds like a good idea," Patrick said, but his face betrayed his lack of enthusiasm. "I think it's a fiercely competitive industry but, as a former small-business advisor, you of all people should be able to determine whether or not it's viable. And you know where to come if you need funding."

"Well, I'll probably buy a second-hand van with my redundancy money and see how it goes. I need something to get about in, now my company car's gone."

Patrick said, "Seriously, if you want a second pair of eyes to go through your business model I'd be happy to oblige."

"Thanks mate. I seem to be thanking you for everything lately, you're proving to be a real pal."

I spent the rest of that morning calling on business acquaintances either in person or on my now fully charged mobile. I also rang a few couriers to enquire about the cost of delivering local packages to get an idea of what they were charging. I checked the Internet for the mpg rates of a few different models of van and current fuel prices. By lunchtime I had two potential customers and the makings of a reasonable business plan.

I'd also discovered that during peak periods, the national courier firms employed owner-drivers on a casual basis. This might be a help to me while I went about building the business. I also made three appointments for that afternoon to see people selling second-hand vans having definitely decided to buy rather than lease. I felt pleased with myself as I popped into Beth's Café for a bite to eat and to maybe persuade her to put some of her business my way too.

The first two vans were very dented and grubby with ridiculously high mileage. The third van, a five-year-old Ford Transit, although a little more than I'd wanted to pay, was in good condition and, despite the 180,000 miles recorded on the clock, the owner was able to produce a full service history and a series of MOT certificates that proved the mileage. We shook hands on the deal and I agreed to sort out insurance and return with the money the next day. The one worrying thing was that all three sellers shook their heads and unanimously told me it was a tough way to make a living. Still, hard work didn't frighten me and I had years of experience watching other start-ups.

The guy I bought from said he'd given up because of back trouble and, when I told him that I'd worked in a bank all my life, he shook his head and advised me to get some training in heavy lifting and join a gym to build up my muscles. I considered myself pretty fit from playing golf every weekend, and felt mildly insulted. I looked forward to telling Patrick all I'd achieved and decided to surprise him by preparing a curry. He got back to the flat with a large cardboard box of groceries and dumped it on the kitchen table. He groaned and placed his palm on the small of his back.

"You should always bend at the knees when putting down heavy boxes, not like you just did from the trunk. No wonder you hurt your back!"

"S...Since when did you become such a b...bloody expert?" Patrick asked.

"I've been educating myself in the library on the techniques of loading and unloading heavy objects," I winked at him then added, "I bought a van this afternoon."

"Blimey, you don't hang about do you?"

"I can't afford to. I need an income if I'm going to help Ella through uni, not to mention paying for a divorce!"

"Is there no hope of reconciliation?" Patrick sounded sad.

I doubted it and shook my head. "I'm not sure I'd want to, even if she did. How could I ever trust her again?"

"Have you thought of marriage guidance counselling?"

Time to change the subject. "I've made us a curry tonight,"

"Smells great!" Patrick called over his shoulder as he went to his room to change out of his work suit.

After a good feast, we sat drinking beer.

Patrick said, "I met Leon Cooper. He made me feel quite uneasy, some of the things he was asking. Care to tell me a bit more about him?"

I pursed my lips, trying to decide how much he needed to know. "He's a very high net worth individual – owns Cooper's Logistics PLC and has fingers in lots of other local businesses too. Quite diverse interests; he even owns a landscape gardening operation, Cooper's Courtyards, which is another lucrative little side line. He's put a lot of business the bank's way over the years and earned me a lot of commission."

"Is he legit?"

"Why do you ask?"

"He was asking me about the banks money laundering triggers and what he had to do to stay under the radar. Got a bit shirty when I said I wasn't allowed to divulge such information. Said you never had any qualms about telling him..." Patrick left the sentence hanging in the air.

I hesitated while I though how best to address his concerns.

"I didn't reveal much about our procedures to him but, as he rightly pointed out, most of his interests are cash businesses and as such, he didn't want to trigger any false alarms that might draw unnecessary police attention to him. I didn't believe, at the time, that he was involved in anything criminal but I did wonder if he was treading a fine line between tax avoidance and evasion."

Patrick leaned forward. "You said 'at the time'. Has anything happened since to change your view?"

Patrick didn't miss a thing.

"Well, an awful lot of money passed through his account and I think he deliberately split it and paid it in over several days just to keep beneath the radar. And he came in once bragging about how he'd 'persuaded' another local businessman, also a client of mine, to sell up even though it clearly wasn't in his best interest. The guy came in the next day with the same banker's draft I'd drawn up for Leon the day before and when he paid it in he looked white as a sheet."

"Do you think Leon coerced him?"

"Yes, I do, but I didn't have a shred of evidence other than the look in the guy's eyes when he paid it in. I saw fear, Patrick. And he'd just sold his business to Leon for about a third of its market value. When I asked him why, he practically ran out of the bank."

"Did you report it?"

"What could I say? I had no evidence to back it up and I sensed that if the previous owner had wanted the police involved he'd have gone to them himself. There must have been some reason for him not to have done so. I'm still not sure Leon actually did anything illegal but he is a ruthless man who likes to have his own way. He isn't the sort of person you'd want to cross as I think he'd make a powerful enemy. So don't upset him is my advice."

"Thanks," Patrick said, and he became very quiet.

CHAPTER SIX

Two days later, I returned to the family home driving my newly acquired white van. When I pulled onto the drive I could see Katrina peering through the window, obviously not recognising the Ford Transit.

She opened the door and said, "You must be at the wrong house we're not expecting a delivery..."

And then she saw me standing there grinning.

Ella came out to see what was happening and threw her arms around me as she always does when she hasn't seen me for a few days.

"What's with the van?" Ella asked.

"This," I said, proudly waving an arm at it, "is my new company car! What do you think?"

"I think you're crazy," she said.

Taking her by the arm I said, "Ella, I have something to tell you."

A look of concern immediately darkened her features.

"It's OK, love, it's nothing to worry about."

Katrina and I had agreed previously over the phone that while we should hide our marital problems from Ella, we should be up-front about the redundancy. I explained my absence by pretending the bank had sent me on a course to set myself up in business.

"...and so here we have my new business venture," I said. Opening the rear door of the van, I withdrew magnetic signs and attached them to the side of the van:

'Martin Blake, Man With A Van – No Job Too Small'

There was also a cartoon caricature of my face on a small body clad in overalls, and my mobile phone number.

Both Ella and Katrina stood open jawed.

Ella seemed pretty cool about the whole idea but soon lost interest and went to her room to play video games and Skype her friends.

It was a different story from Katrina though. As soon as we were alone she turned on me and said, "Have you gone completely mad? How much money did you waste on that awful van and how are you going to make any money as a van driver?"

"I've looked into it and I'm working on my business plan and what's more I already have three customers who've promised to put some work my way!"

"How can you possibly expect to compete for business with the likes of the Royal Mail? This is madness, Martin! And where do you think you're going to keep the van because I'm not having it on our drive! What will the neighbours think?"

I felt the blood rush to my face. "Do you think I give a shit what the bloody neighbours think?" I said, growling the words in an attempt to keep my voice low enough for Ella not to hear.

"They'll complain; you know they will. There's even something in the deeds about not parking commercial vehicles on this estate."

"So bloody what, let them complain; we'll be selling the damn place soon enough anyway."

"Keep your voice down," Katrina hissed. As my words sank in she looked nonplussed.

"I want to keep the house," she said.

"And how do you propose to buy out my half?" I was

sneering now – I couldn't help it.

"I am not going to discuss this with you, especially while Ella's around. And not even after that. We'll negotiate through solicitors."

I took a long breath, "You've already instructed a solicitor?"

"I have an appointment with Lammerton and Williams on Monday morning at ten o'clock."

The finality of what she said struck me hard.

"Don't give me your lost-puppy-look," she said, "it'll be easier if we do it through solicitors, you know it will."

*

I sat in the doorway of my shed, puffing a much-needed cigar and wondered how the hell I was going to get through the next fortnight. And how we were going to break the news to my beautiful Ella who, although she was practically grown up, would always be my little girl. How on earth would she react?

We managed to get through the meal, letting Ella do most of the talking. If she did sense any strain between her parents she showed no sign.

"I'm going to the cinema with Sally and Chloe tonight," she announced.

"Shouldn't you be revising? Your first exam is on Monday isn't it?"

"Mum, I've been revising all week. I have to have some breaks and it's English on Monday, my best subject."

"Well, I expect you to do some more revision over the weekend – this is your last chance remember and if you don't put the work in and get the grades you need, you won't get the university place you want."

"I'll run you in if you like, in the new van," I offered, glad of an excuse to get out of the house. I wasn't sure I could cope with an evening alone with Katrina.

"That'd be cool!" said Ella.

She enjoyed having such a high up view of the road and bubbled with enthusiasm that I was going into business for myself.

"If anyone can make a go of it, you can Dad," she said.

I felt touched by her positivity and unconditional faith in my abilities. It felt wonderful to have someone who believed in me so utterly and completely. If I was going to make a success of this venture then I'd be doing it as much for her as for myself.

I didn't feel inclined to hurry back and drove the van twenty-odd miles to Ogmore-by-Sea just to watch the sun sink slowly over the horizon while I smoked another cigar; I'd been trying to give them up. Who wasn't these days? I'd managed to keep to two a day until the events of this week made me reach for the packet at every opportunity. I'd have to watch it, but, what the hell, I needed something to get me through these difficult times.

I got home at about ten o'clock. Ella was still out and, much as she admired her Dad's new van, she didn't want me to pick her up in front of her mates and said one of their dads had already offered them a lift back.

Katrina greeted me with the cold words, "I've made up the spare bed for you."

"Don't you think Ella might suspect something if we suddenly start sleeping in separate rooms?"

"I'll tell her I'm not sleeping well and having headaches, and that you very kindly agreed to sleep in the spare room so I could have the light on if needs be without disturbing you."

"I thought we didn't want to worry her just before her exams. Don't you think your being ill might worry her just a little too?"

"I'll tell her it's just my time of the month and nothing to worry about."

"You seem to have it all worked out," I said. "Lying comes so easily to you these days!"

Katrina glowered at me but ignored the jibe. Instead she said, "I'm tired. Will you wait up for Ella?"

I nodded. I'd always waited up for her, sometimes until

two in the morning. I could never settle until I knew she was safely indoors. She'd complained at first but was used to it now and would be expecting me to be awake. Just like always, I thought and again felt a twinge of fear at what the future might hold.

I didn't care about the sleeping arrangements; in fact, I'd already wondered how I would feel about sleeping in the bed where I'd caught them having sex. I was shocked that she already had an appointment to see a solicitor. I hadn't really factored the cost of a divorce anywhere in my business plan and wondered how much it would be. Katrina had chosen to stay at home to bring up Ella and she'd probably have a claim on my pension and maybe even try to take half my redundancy payout. I swallowed a build up of saliva and it went the wrong way making me cough violently. I would need to talk to a solicitor soon too. I was under no illusions about what could happen, having seen at first hand the effect divorce had on some of my clients' bank accounts.

CHAPTER SEVEN

Somehow, we managed to get through the next two weeks without fighting in front of Ella. If she had noticed we were sleeping in separate rooms she didn't question it and, because no explanation was called for, we didn't have to pretend one of us had a cold. Much to our great relief, she hadn't even stirred when Tim's wife threw a brick through our window and was subsequently bundled off to stay with her mother. Indeed, Ella was so preoccupied with her exams and her own teenage dramas that I doubted she'd have noticed anything much short of the house exploding.

Katrina and I managed to rub along without too much trouble mainly because we carefully avoided being in the same room as one another most of the time. Both of us now had solicitors and Katrina had come to accept that we'd have to sell the house. In any case, she graciously conceded she didn't feel she wanted to live in this house with Tim. Bitch. If Katrina had been in contact with Tim, and I assume she must have been, then she was being incredibly discreet about it. I tried not to dwell upon how expertly she'd concealed the affair from me.

To keep from thinking about it too much, I threw myself into setting up my business and quickly realised that making a living as a van driver was going to be much tougher than I thought. Most of the businesses I tried already had reliable arrangements in place and were reluctant to take a chance on someone new. Where they did agree to use me they knocked me down to such a low price that I was barely able to cover the cost of petrol, which seemed to be increasing at the pumps on an almost daily basis.

I didn't fare much better with the national firms. They all said they employed casual owner-drivers and that they would call me if any work came in. But my phone remained ominously silent.

Most of the second week I spent looking for somewhere to rent until I could sort my finances out. The trouble was the only places I could afford tended to be in the more seedy areas of the city. The harsh reality of my situation was beginning to sink in and I didn't much like it.

Finally, Ella's exams were over and while she refused to give any indication about how she felt they'd gone, it was clear from her demeanour that they couldn't have thrown up too many problems. We let her go out to celebrate on the Friday evening and agreed we would sit her down and break the news to her on Saturday morning.

Katrina had initially wanted to keep Tim out of any discussions but I insisted that if Ella asked if anyone else was involved she should be completely open and honest with her.

*

Ella stayed in bed most of the morning, presumably nursing a bad head – I'd waited up for her until three o'clock in the morning and helped her totter happily and noisily up the stairs, neither of us caring if we woke her mother. I wondered how hungover she'd be when she eventually awoke to hear our news.

We both felt nervous about what we had to say to her. Finally, we heard sounds coming from upstairs and exchanged worried glances as the shower was turned on.

Ella emerged twenty minutes later in a dressing gown with a towel tied turban-style around her head. Before getting down to the matter in hand we politely listened to her bubbling enthusiasm about the 'wicked' party she'd had. She showed no signs of being hungover and I couldn't help, once again, longing to be the age where hangovers just went away in the night like that.

I asked her to sit down on the sofa opposite us and said, "Ella, we've got something to tell you."

"Blimey," she said, looking suddenly worried, "this sounds serious. What have I done?"

"You've done absolutely nothing wrong my love, but your Mum and I have something to tell you..."

I began to falter, so Katrina took over, coming straight to the point, "We wanted to wait until after you'd completed your examinations," she said, "but, the fact is, your father and I have realised we no longer love each other and we've decided it would be best if we separated."

Even to me, her words sounded so final and I couldn't help wondering where we'd gone so wrong that we lost all the love we'd shared. I felt a lump form in my throat and forced myself to swallow – I couldn't lose control, not now.

Ella went quiet and pale, her eyes darting from one to the other of us. "When you say separated, you mean divorced?

"Yes, it will be permanent," said Katrina.

"But how can you both just stop loving each other?" Ella's voice rose to a whine, as she mirrored my own thoughts.

I could see she was fighting to hold it together and realised we were right to let her get the exams out of the way. She was taking it hard.

"We didn't just suddenly stop loving one another," I said, "in fact, we still do love each other on some level."

I looked across at Katrina, for confirmation and felt relieved to see her nod, she added "We'll always love each other as friends and we'll both still be there for you as parents. It's just that we've gradually grown apart and reached the point where living together is making us unhappy."

"Is that why you've been sleeping in separate rooms?" Ella asked, surprising us both.

Katrina and I looked at one another.

"I'm not stupid, you know," Ella said, "I do notice things around here, but I can hardly ask my parents 'Hey why aren't you two sleeping together anymore?' What was I supposed to say?"

Ella looked from one to the other of us and then turned her eyes towards the carpet, falling silent.

I was lost for words. Katrina seemed to be thinking hard. She looked like she was about to speak when Ella looked at us with pleading eyes and said, "I still don't understand why you have to separate. Can't you both try and rekindle your love somehow? Surely love doesn't just stop like that?"

"You're right, Ella, it doesn't just 'stop like that'," Katrina said. "One of us has become..." she cleared her throat and appeared to choose the next word carefully, "...'involved' with someone else."

Ella looked accusingly at me. "You?" she said, her voice rising in anger, "how could you do that to Mum?"

I shook my head, aghast that she could even think it was me.

Katrina cleared her throat and mumbled, "It was me."

"What did you say?" Ella looked outraged.

Katrina repeated herself in a slightly louder voice. Her face had gone white.

Ella turned to me and I saw something like pity in her eyes, or maybe it was empathy, I wasn't really sure which but it made me feel weak and ashamed.

"I'm sorry, Ella," Katrina said. She looked strained and I noticed dark rings under her eyes.

"Well it's not me you should be apologising to!" Ella

said, nodding her head in my direction, "God Mum! How could you?"

Then something else dawned on her intelligent features.

"Has this got anything to do with that woman down the road throwing a brick through our window a couple of weeks ago?" she asked.

Katrina's jaw dropped, "We thought you'd slept right through that. You didn't say anything!"

"I did sleep right through it! But a couple of days later, Chloe overheard two women gossiping in the newsagents where she works. I felt really stupid not knowing anything about it!"

"We didn't say anything because we didn't want to distract you from your exams, that's all," Katrina said.

Then Ella reverted back to a whining voice that I hadn't heard since she was just a little girl as she asked, "What's going to happen to me if you two are splitting up? Where will I go?"

My heart went out to her.

"Nothing will happen to the house before you go into digs at uni in the autumn," Katrina said.

"But what about the holidays? Where do I come home to? What am I supposed to do with all my stuff?"

"Wherever we end up living, I know I speak for both of us when I say there will always be a room for you," Katrina said, looking to me for confirmation.

I said, "Don't worry love, it's all a bit uncertain now but it'll work out; I promise you."

Ella took a tissue from her pocket and put it to her nose. Then she abruptly rose and made for the door.

Katrina tried to take her arm but Ella knocked her hand away and said, "Don't touch me!" before slamming the door behind her.

I got up to follow her.

"Leave her be, for now," Katrina urged, "she's had a shock and needs to take it in. She's a bright girl, she'll come to terms with it. Just give her time."

Katrina's shoulders sagged and she seemed to shrink into the armchair. "What if she never speaks to me again?" she said, her despair evident on her face.

My own emotions were in turmoil too. Part of me wanted to reach out and comfort her and tell her we could work things out, but another, more spiteful, side of me felt like saying see what you've brought upon yourself!

In the end I said nothing. I just walked away and took refuge in the garden, unsure I'd ever come to terms with it myself. I noticed the curtains of Ella's bedroom were drawn, shutting out the sun. I felt I was letting her down so badly and I hated myself for it.

CHAPTER EIGHT

Business was slow. I reminded myself that most start-up businesses made a loss in the first year and tried to shut out of my mind the number of start-ups I'd seen fail. I'd discussed my business plans with Patrick and he gently pointed out some of the realities. I decided not to saddle the business with a large debt to start, choosing instead to use a chunk of my redundancy money, partly influenced by a nagging thought that if I didn't spend it fast, Katrina would get her claws into it.

Despite promising to behave like adults and remain friends, things between us were becoming strained as we wrangled about the finances, even though it was mostly at arm's length through our solicitors.

I moved into a cheap bedsit in Grangetown until it was all sorted and I could find somewhere better. It was not a great area of Cardiff, and on the second morning some low-life had broken into my van and stolen the radio and the small trolley I kept in the back. The radio I could make do without, but I had to replace the trolley and spend a few hundred fixing the damage caused by a jemmy to the rear doors. I also invested in a sticker that proclaimed 'No Valuables Left In This Vehicle Overnight'.

That morning I had a catering delivery for Beth's Café and cheerfully flicked on my hazards and double-parked right outside the place, just as I'd learned from the driver I'd replaced and much to the annoyance of other motorists.

"Morning Sunshine." Beth greeted me like an old friend now. True to her word, she'd let me have all her local deliveries, admitting that she hadn't much liked the fellow who'd done her deliveries before because there was 'something shifty' about him.

In the kitchen at the back Beth took me to one side and in low tones said, "Watch your back today Martin; the previous delivery driver is in having a coffee and he was asking about you. He wanted to know if you were undercutting him. He didn't like it much when I told him I wouldn't discuss your business with him any more than I would have told you about his business."

I shrugged, "He should know it's nothing personal, it's just the way of the world."

"All the same," Beth said, "keep your eyes open. He might be the type to cause trouble for you."

"Thanks Beth. What about you, is he likely to give you any grief?"

"Don't worry about me, I can look after myself." Beth picked up a handy rolling pin and brandished it but she looked more like a cartoon granny than a serious threat.

When I walked back through the shop I looked across to the man's table. He wore his hair in a long greasy ponytail that protruded from the back of the same grubby red baseball cap I'd seen before. It was obvious why Beth wasn't happy about this scruffy, unhygienic little man delivering food. He openly glowered at me as I passed and then made a big show of writing something in a small notebook.

I'd barely driven a hundred yards when my phone rang with a withheld number.

Although the tiny speaker made everyone sound tinny,

there was no mistaking the malice in the voice that issued forth and seemed to fill the small cab.

"I'll 'ave yer, yer bastard!" said Mr Ponytail from the café.

Before I could respond, he ended the call. I wasn't going to allow such a pathetic little man to intimidate me. If the coward had been serious then surely he'd have confronted me outside the cafe. I forced myself to whistle a happy tune and forget all about him.

∗

The next day, all my deliveries were done by lunchtime so I decided to ring a few of the big firms again to see if I could pick up any casual owner-driver jobs. One of the supervisors, a guy named Luke, said there might be something for me the following day and that he'd ring me back later to confirm. They didn't pay much – about £1 a parcel – which wasn't going to leave much room for profit but it was a foot in the door and I felt optimistic.

When my phone rang a few minutes later, I snatched it up enthusiastically and said, "Hello, Martin Blake here. Is that Luke?"

The voice at the other end of the line hesitated. "Uh, is that the Man with a Van? I saw your advert in the local paper, no job too small..."

I'd looked into placing advertisements in the local press but decided it was too expensive for the time being – he must've picked up my ad in the free-press.

"That's right," I said. "What can I do for you, sir?"

The man sounded elderly and his breath was laboured, "I bought a bicycle on the Internet for my grandson and the idiots delivered it to my address instead of my grandson's. I told them to take it to him but they refused, saying they had too many other deliveries to make today and if they took it back and got it reassigned then he wouldn't get it in time for his birthday, which is tomorrow. I know it's short notice but can you take it from me and deliver it safely to him in time for tomorrow? I'm too old to be trying to lift big boxes and besides, it'll never fit in my little car." The man began coughing and wheezing.

I was disgusted at the attitude of the couriers towards such an obviously frail old man.

I asked whereabouts he lived and the correct delivery address and quoted what I felt was a fair price.

"That'll be fine," the man said. "How soon can you get here?"

"About forty-five minutes, allowing for traffic."

"Marvellous! Now do you have a satnav because I'm quite hard to find."

The man said he lived in Draethen, an area to the northeast of Cardiff. He gave me the coordinates and said, "Now you can't see my house from the road but when you get to the Forestry Commission land you'll see what looks like a dirt track going into the forest. Take that track – it winds around a few bends for a couple of hundred yards and then you'll see my house in a clearing on the right hand side. You got that?"

I repeated the instructions and said I was on my way.

Just as I picked up my keys the phone rang again. This time it was Luke from the depot. I'd need to be there at six AM sharp as all drivers, contract and permanent had to go through some health and safety training before being allowed out for the first time.

Two new clients in one day, things were looking up.

*

The old man was right, the place was hard to find and I'd almost certainly have driven past the turning if I hadn't been given such precise instructions. The track was uneven and narrow in places and I hoped the tangled undergrowth at the edge of the path wouldn't scratch the van. The path didn't seem much used and I wondered what kind of property the old man must be living in. Perhaps he was a retired forester or something. Although the city was less than five miles as the crow flies, the remote loneliness of such a place would never appeal to me. I much preferred to have people and houses around me than trees. Still, I thought, each to their own.

The track twisted uphill and I wondered how many more sharp bends I'd have to take before reaching the old man's property. The track was narrow too with passing places about every hundred yards or so. I could hear an engine running elsewhere in the forest but it may have just been traffic passing on the road below. I really didn't want to meet something coming the other way as, although I was getting used to driving the van, it was much larger than the saloons I'd driven all my life and I still struggled reversing only using wing mirrors.

I rounded the next bend and came face to face with a big black 4x4 off-road vehicle. Thankfully, the other driver must have heard me coming because he was waiting just next to a convenient passing place. Relieved, I pulled into the lay-by to allow the other vehicle to pass. The windows were tinted and the low angle of the sun slanting through the trees made it impossible for me to see the other driver. Instead of passing, the vehicle stopped completely blocking me in and someone got out of the passenger side and walked around the back. I couldn't see much of him but I could tell he was tall and well-built.

I heard the driver's door open but my eyes were fixed on the big guy who I now saw was smacking a big iron crowbar into the palm of his hand.

I swallowed hard as I caught sight in the wing mirror of a familiar grubby red baseball hat.

After that things moved fast and yet seemed to be happening in slow motion.

I tried to operate the central locking but I was too late.

There was a loud smash and the windscreen splintered into tiny squares and fell into my lap. The impact triggered the airbag which slapped into my face, stunning me. My door was yanked open, and I felt hands grabbing my arm and thigh and pulling me out of the cab. It was the man in the baseball cap, and he flung me roughly to the ground and kicked me hard in my side. I rolled away in agony wondering if a rib was broken.

The pain made me gasp for breath but the blows kept coming with a terrifying savagery. I curled into the foetus position but that didn't help me much as the kicker simply switched his attention to my kidneys. I heard ringing in my ears, punctuated by the sound of breaking glass as the man with the crowbar methodically smashed everything that would break on the van. I prayed that he wasn't going start on me when he'd finished on the van because one blow from that thing would surely kill me. Baseball-cap man was still kicking and punching me and yelling "This'll teach yer!" with every blow that rained down on me. I felt hands rolling me over to face the other way and then watched helplessly as a trainer-clad foot stamped on my face.

Then it was all over, stopping as suddenly as it had started. The men retreated into the 4x4 and I heard the engine rev and the tyres scrunch the gravel track just a few feet from my head. I looked up and sensed rather than saw that someone else inside the vehicle was gazing out at me from the back through the tinted glass.

As it pulled away slowly I tried to lift my head to get the number plate but my sight was too blurred and then my head dropped back onto the floor.

*

I wasn't sure how long I'd lain there. It must have been a few hours because dusk had arrived in the forest. Flashing blue lights and arc lamps made shadows dance around me. Someone was bending over me shining a bright light in my eyes which I flinched away from.

I heard a voice say, "He's coming around."

Gradually, I became aware of others searching the ground nearby with flashlights.

"It's OK, sir. The ambulance is here, my name is Warren, I'm a paramedic and I'm going to give you an injection in a minute to ease the pain. But first I need to ask you some questions. Let's start with an easy one: what's your name?"

I tried to raise my head to answer and it felt like I'd been kicked again. I tried to speak but my voice was hoarse and my throat dry so when I spoke my name it came out, "Marrin..."

"Was that Martin?"

"...'es."

"OK Martin, I'm going to gently touch different parts of your limbs and body and I want you to just grunt if you can feel where I'm touching you. Do you understand?"

I grunted.

I felt the paramedic's hands gently prodding and exploring my body and grunted an acknowledgement every time. When the man touched my side it made me wince in pain.

"OK, a little bit sore there are we?"

I grunted another affirmation at this gross understatement of my agony.

"Right, I'm going to give you a painkiller now. You'll just feel a tiny prick in your arm and then we'll get you to hospital and make you more comfortable."

I felt the needle and then a coolness spread up my left arm and throughout my body, sweeping my pain away like driftwood on the tide.

*

The next time I awoke I was in a hospital bed with a drip in my arm and various bits of equipment beeping near to me.

I ached from head to toe and whenever I tried to draw a deep breath or move I felt a sharp pain in my side. Consequently, I stayed as still as I could and kept my breathing shallow. I opened my eyes and found Katrina sitting in a seat next to the bed. I was so relieved to see her, even though she looked drawn, and I think I momentarily forgot we were no longer a team.

"God, Martin you look awful. What happened? What were you doing in the middle of a forest?"

I tried to speak but ended up just shaking my head, I couldn't answer her questions yet.

"I'd better tell the nurse you're awake," she said, rising from her chair.

She returned with a pretty young nurse who didn't look much older than Ella.

"Hello Mr Blake," she said, cheerfully. "I'm Karen and I'm going to be looking after you today. Are you comfortable? Would you like something to drink, a glass of water perhaps?"

"Water, please," I gasped.

The nurse poured me a plastic beaker of water from a jug on the bedside table and brought it to my lips, gently lifting my head from the pillow so I could take a sip.

The cool water eased its way down my throat.

"There's a policeman waiting to see you," said Karen, "but you don't have to talk to him until you're ready to and the doctor has insisted he sees you first just to check you're ok."

The doctor arrived about ten minutes later and told me that, apart from a cracked rib, no bones were broken and most of my pain was coming from a few cuts and bruises. He wanted to keep me in overnight, purely for observation, in case I suffered from any delayed concussion or shock. He told me that tomorrow, all being well, I could go home and rest. There was nothing to prescribe except strong painkillers. He offered to write a sick note and it dawned on me suddenly that, being self-employed, no one was going to pay me for being off sick like the bank had – welcome to the real world I thought.

After the doctor left, Katrina said she had some shopping to do and left me to rest. "Do you want me to return with Ella during visiting hours this evening?" she asked.

"I don't want her to be upset by the sight of me," I said, although really I so wanted to see her.

"I'll bring her with me – she'll be even more worried if

she doesn't see you."

She got up and the effort of grabbing her hand made me wince. "Katrina," I said in a whisper, "thanks for coming."

She didn't answer but just patted the back of my hand and quietly left.

I'd barely closed my eyes when nurse Karen popped in to remind me the policeman was still waiting.

A young detective constable called Sam Jeffries asked me to tell him everything I could remember, which wasn't much really. He wrote everything down and said they'd follow up on the driver with the red baseball cap but he gave a doubtful shrug suggesting it probably wouldn't come to much.

"You've had a professional beating," he told me as he got up to leave. "They let you off lightly; just a cracked rib and a few bruises. – You're lucky, it could have been a lot worse."

I didn't feel lucky, not at all! I'd never been 'beaten up' in my life, not even as a schoolboy. Although I'd always been tall and quite rugged-looking I had a natural aversion to hurting myself. In school, I'd carefully avoided contact sports like rugby and even football, favouring athletics. I developed strategies to avoid fights by befriending the right people and although I inevitably had the odd scrap, the only thing still hurting the next day was my pride. I'd taken these skills into my adult life and my ability to get on with people had led me into sales in the bank.

"What about my van?" I asked.

"It's not roadworthy in its current condition but, just like yourself, the damage is mostly superficial by the looks of it. All the windows were smashed and the wing mirrors and the panels took a few dents and scratches too. It'll cost a bit to put right mind, and I'd get the garage to check they didn't put any sugar in your fuel tank before starting the engine, just in case. We put it on a low-loader and it'll stay in our secure compound until you settle the recovery costs and organise collection."

"Thanks," I said, allowing my head to flop back on the pillow. I couldn't help wondering how much all this was going to cost my struggling new business.

A nurse came later and removed the drip from my arm and the monitoring equipment and I rose stiffly from my bed to make my own way to the toilet. There was a mirror in there and I caught sight of myself and gasped. Both my eyes were just purple slits. My lips felt like rubber and I could see one of my front crowns was missing. I ran a finger along a line of shallow abrasions on my cheek and, in horror, I realised they formed a match with the pattern on the sole of the trainer that had stomped on my face.

"You're *lucky*!" I told my reflection and then slowly turned my back, not wanting to look any more.

CHAPTER NINE

It took a week and half to get the van back on the road and for the bruises to subside enough so that I no longer scared small children. I couldn't afford to do any repairs beyond making the van roadworthy so the dents in the panelling remained, making 'the man and his van' look as though life had been hard. Not really the business appearance I'd been aiming at.

I'd thought long and hard about whether to heed the warnings, or continue in spite of them. In the end, it was partly a lack of any other ideas about what I might do and partly a kind of new determination set in me not to be beaten or bullied out of my business venture. I scaled back on my private clientele however, choosing instead the relative safety of contract work with the national firms. I got used to setting my alarm for a five o'clock start and soon earned a reputation as a hard, reliable worker. I usually finished by the middle of the afternoon, having delivered anywhere between 150 and 200 packages ranging in size from CDs and DVDs to large heavy boxes. At a flat rate of £1 per delivery, I wasn't making a lot after overheads but it was a steady income and covered the rent and living costs. It was also having a profound effect on my physique; I'd shed over 11lbs and my muscles were developing some tone. Physically I hadn't been this good a shape since my days as a squash player.

The police had occasionally been in touch, but they had no real leads and I sensed they were losing interest. Then, one Wednesday morning three weeks after the attack, I received a call from a Detective Sergeant Bryn Williams.

DS Williams was a big bear of a man with a broken nose of a boxer and the flattened ears of a rugby player. I was glad we were on the same side.

"Any joy?" I asked as soon as we were alone.

"Nothing as yet, Mr Blake, but we're still working on it, I promise you. What we would like you to do today is go through these mugshots and see if you can identify any of the men that attacked you."

He left me sitting at a computer screen scrolling through photo after photo and told me to give a shout if I spotted anyone. After about twenty minutes he popped his head around the door and asked if I'd like a coffee, by which time my eyes were already glazed with boredom.

Were they expecting me to scroll through the whole national police database?

Suddenly a face flashed up that I thought might be the man who'd wielded the crowbar. It was difficult from just the head and shoulders shot to get a feeling for the size of the man, but I felt it *could* be him. This breakthrough of sorts renewed my enthusiasm for the task although I was flagging again after another fifteen minutes. I was bombing through the photos by now, just allowing a few seconds to stare at each one, keen to reach the end of the job. Then another face popped in front of me: I had to scroll back through three screens to find it again once it had registered in my brain.

"Bingo!" I cried. As soon as the face filled the screen I was absolutely certain it was the man in the baseball hat. His hair was shorter and instead of being tied in a ponytail it was loose over his ears but it was definitely him. I immediately called for DS Williams.

"Ah, you know, I thought it might be him," he said.

"Well if you thought that why didn't you just show me his photo first instead of making me plough through all those others?" I felt peeved.

"Because we're not allowed to lead the witnesses," Williams replied with a grin, "otherwise the court might rule it inadmissible, see."

I found myself beginning to warm to this burly Welshman with the twinkle in his eye. I showed him the other photo.

"I think this might be the man with the crowbar," I said, "but I'm not so certain as I didn't get much of a look at him."

Williams looked thoughtful, "Hmmm, it may have been him. These two are known associates.

"You've done well, Mr Blake. Thank you very much for your time today and your patience. We'll look into the whereabouts of these two and keep you posted."

*

Although it was taking a risk, I still did deliveries for Beth's Café. She'd asked me to deliver catering supplies to a large house in Lisvane, an upmarket suburb of Cardiff. The owner of one of the walled mansions lining the road had installed a marquee in the grounds for his daughter's wedding reception. The address seemed familiar but I couldn't think why.

At the gate of what turned out to be quite a mansion, I had to press an intercom to be let in. I was directed to the rear of the property and after I'd unloaded all the boxes into the marquee a surly man in a dark suit said, "Follow me please, the boss wants to see you." He didn't wait for a reply, abruptly turning on his heels.

I was curious to see what kind of man owned a place like this.

He led me across a decked area with expensive garden furniture, through a door into a kitchen the size of the whole floor area of my flat and then into an equally massive hall with a balustrade staircase that lead to a gallery landing. A scale model of the Eiffel Tower, taller than me, stood in a corner. My feet sank into the carpet making me wonder if I should've removed the industrial steel-toe-capped boots that I'd started wearing for health and safety.

The man held a door open for me but didn't follow me through it.

The room had a distinctly French feel. Impressionist paintings adorned the walls. One I recognised, a copy surely, was by Monet. Another one, more gruesome, depicted a pile of skulls. Three comfortable looking antique Chesterfields made a U-shape around a fireplace that could have once been in a stately home. I immediately recognised the wavy hair of the familiar figure that rose to greet me. Leon Cooper grinned at me – although I'd never been to his home, how could I not have recognised his address? He held out his hand and I braced myself for his familiar vice-like grip.

"It's a wonderful place you have here," I said, waving my arm at our surroundings until my gaze rested on a painting of skulls above his fireplace.

"Do you like it?" he asked, "It's called Pyramid of Skulls and was painted by Paul Cézanne between 1898 and 1905. My mother was French and she taught me such a lot about art."

"I had no idea you were an art lover," I said, slowly recovering from my initial surprise.

"When it comes down to it, we really know so little about our acquaintances, Martin."

He inspected the bruises on my face and shook his head sadly. He said, "Thank you for making the time to see me; come and sit down. Would you like a cigar? They're made from 100% French tobacco grown in the foothills of the Pyrenees."

He held out a wooden box of cigars bearing the name

Navarre. I could see they were way more expensive than the cheap panatelas I smoked. It was tempting although I said "No thanks," but then I couldn't resist his offer of a fine malt whiskey. When I saw the size of the cut-glass in Leon's hand, I said, "Better make it a small one – I'm driving!"

"I heard that stupid short-sighted new manager at the bank made you redundant," Leon said. "Tell me, Martin, why didn't you come to me for help?"

"It wouldn't occur to me to go to anyone with a begging bowl. Besides, as you know, I've spent most of my career advising local businessmen and I wanted to give something completely different a try."

"So you decided to go into the courier business," Leon said, "in direct competition with me."

He met my eye, the edge in his voice unmistakable.

"I hardly think my small one-man-and-his-van operation is going to compete with a business the size and scale of Cooper Logistics." I forced myself to remain calm and held Leon's cold blue eyes. I put what I hoped looked like a self-deprecating smile on my face.

"We all start small," Leon said, "but you've picked an overcrowded and competitive market. And, as those bruises on your face testify, people get very protective of their beats."

Was I being warned off again? I chose to remain silent until I had a better idea where this was heading.

Leon continued "The man who did this..."

"...Is known to the police and it'll only be a matter of time before they pick him up." I interrupted.

"There's a world of difference between being known to the police," Leon paused to puff his cigar, "and being 'picked up' by them. Anyway, I was going to say, the man who did this worked for me, well... he used to. He overstepped the mark and misinterpreted my instructions. Since leaving my employment he's gone away from the district so I assure you he'll not be bothering you anymore."

I felt perplexed. Had Leon just as good as admitted he'd asked this man to warn me off, but had then sacked him for going in too hard? I knew that in business Leon was an ends-justifies-means kind of guy and that he sometimes blurred the boundaries. That's why I'd warned Patrick to be wary. But having me beaten up?

He took a bulky window envelope out of his inside pocket, placing it on the coffee table between us and said, "Please put this towards the repair of your van."

I could see bank notes through the window of the envelope but remained still. "That's very kind of you to offer, Leon, but I really can't accept your money. It doesn't seem right that you should have to pay for something you didn't do."

I left the words hanging in the space between us.

"Please take it," he said, pushing the envelope further towards me, "the man was an employee of mine and I feel some accountability for his actions. Please do not offend me by refusing my gift."

The truth was I couldn't really afford to turn the money down, but neither did I want to be beholden to this man.

Sensing my hesitation, Leon pushed the envelope closer until it balanced on the edge of the table. "Believe me, the amount in here is nothing compared to the money you've made me over the years with your shrewd investment advice. And let me assure you that this gift will place you under no obligation to me. If you were still at the bank, then of course you couldn't accept this – but now you're a free agent you can do whatever you choose."

It was true I'd helped make good investments for Leon and it was all pretty much above board. I picked up the envelope stuffing it into my inside pocket. I could see a £50 note through the envelope window and from the weight there must be at least £1000 inside.

"Thanks," I said.

"My pleasure," he said, beaming at me.

I began to rise from the chair, assuming the meeting had come to an end, but he waved at me to remain seated.

"Please," he said, "if you could just grant me a little more of your time I've a proposition for you. But, as I said, I don't want you to feel under any obligation."

I sat back down.

"Now that I've dispensed with the man who did this terrible thing to you, I need to replace him with another driver."

"Oh, I don't think I could..." I began to protest.

"Wait, please hear me out. What I'm looking for is much more than to just replace a van driver. I need someone intelligent, trustworthy and above all, reliable. Someone who can think in a crisis and make sensible decisions on the spot without always having to refer back to me for guidance. In short, Martin, someone like you."

"I don't know, Leon."

I was already certain I really didn't want to work for this man.

"We haven't talked salary yet," he said. "I'll match whatever you were earning at the bank plus ten percent on top and I promise you will also earn regular bonuses far greater than anything you've been paid before."

"But you could pay at least two full-time drivers for what I was taking home at the bank!"

"I know," said Leon.

He told me a little more about how he envisaged my role as a kind of trouble-shooter.

"May I have time to think this over?" I asked.

He became irritated and abruptly stood up.

"No," he said, "the man I need for the job must be able to make decisions on the spot and act upon them. If you need time to think about it then you're not the man I thought you were. The deal is on the table now, take it or walk away and forget about it."

I swallowed hard as a distant voice barely recognisable as my own said, "In that case, it's a very kind offer, Leon, and I thank you from the bottom of my heart but I really want to be my own boss right now so I must decline."

I'm not sure if outside a cloud floated across the sun but inside I swear the room darkened.

He gave a flicker of a smile before saying, "So be it, Martin. I wish you good luck, my friend." Then he turned and left the room, leaving his men to usher me out.

CHAPTER TEN

When I returned to the flat, my tea was interrupted by a knock at the door. Although we'd never actually spoken, I recognised the lanky Rastafarian who lived in the apartment above me. He looked intimidating until he broke into a big friendly, bright-eyed smile.

"My name's Marley," he said, in a broad Jamaican accent. "I live upstairs."

We shook hands and I said, "Hi Marley, good to meet you."

I wasn't sure whether or not to invite him in and he filled an awkward moment by telling me, almost apologetically, "My ma was a big reggae fan so she called me older brother Bob and I got stuck with Marley."

"Well it could've been worse," I said, "she might have been a Bob Geldof fan."

He smiled politely then said, "Look, I'm sorry to bother you man but I thought you should know I just chased off a couple of guys who were messing about under your van. I think they may have been after your cat."

"I don't have a cat," I said, with a frown.

He roared at this and slapped his thigh. "You're funny, man" he said. "I mean they were after your catalytic converter: it's worth a couple of hundred quid as scrap and they're fairly easy to steal off vans like yours - happens all de time. Thing is, now they know it's there they'll probably be back so you may wanna think about finding a lock-up, you know what I'm saying, man?"

"Thanks, Marley, I appreciate that. Do you want to come in for a beer?"

"No thanks, man, just being neighbourly that's all. Good to meet ya!"

After he'd gone I went outside to double check the van. The underside looked OK to me and I thanked my lucky stars that Marley had happened along. I glanced up and down the road but it was deserted and my guess was, whoever they were, they wouldn't be back tonight as they'd alerted us. I added 'find secure parking' to my mental checklist for tomorrow and returned inside.

Much later, long after I'd gone to bed and fallen asleep, I was woken by someone beating on my door. There was a flickering orange light around the edges of my curtains and the acrid smell of smoke filled the room.

I opened the door to find Marley standing in gold-coloured pyjamas clutching a fire extinguisher which he waved in my face. "Grab yours and follow me, man," he yelled, "your van's on fire!"

I picked up the extinguisher from my kitchen and followed him outside. The cab of the van was already ablaze with black smoke blotting out any stars in the night sky. There was a loud crackling noise interspersed with pops and bangs as things inside melted and caught alight. The fire already had a good hold at the front of the van as Marley and I tried in vain to get close enough to set off our puny extinguishers. We may as well have been using water pistols for all the difference they made in the few seconds they took to empty. Lights were coming on in neighbouring properties and one bare-chested man dashed out with a bucket of water, flung it on the fire and then ran back for another.

"We need to call the fire brigade!" I shouted at Marley.

"Already done it, mate," yelled the bucket-man over his shoulder. "They're on their way!"

More neighbours appeared and Marley organised them to form a human chain and soon buckets of water began passing hand-to-hand down the line. I felt a little surprised and very proud of the way the community was coming to my rescue. I was nearest the van and could see the buckets weren't coming nearly fast enough to have any material affect on the inferno. But what else could we do?

The bright orange flames were leaping ten feet into the air now and the heat became so intense it was driving us further away. A tyre popped and hissed as the air burst out and the van lurched dangerously to one side. For a second, I thought it was going to topple onto me.

"We need to get back," I shouted above the roar, "the petrol tank might explode any minute!"

I tried to think what the fuel gauge had been reading when I parked and guessed it must still be at least a quarter full.

At last, sirens could be heard as the fire engine drew closer. It had taken them just minutes but it felt like an eternity to me as I watched helplessly while my business dreams went up in smoke.

Finally, blue lights stabbed through the air and the siren stopped abruptly. Had it been during the day I'm sure the column of black smoke would have cast a long shadow over Grangetown. Firemen in yellow helmets emerged calmly from the tender and set efficiently about their business. The man who took charge verified that no one was inside the vehicle as he ushered us further back. The police had also arrived and were busy evacuating nearby properties and stopping traffic. Two firemen approached the burning vehicle with a hose. The thick jet of water hissed as it struck the hot metal and the black smoke instantly turned steamy white. At first, the flames seemed to resist the onslaught but gradually they succumbed. Paint had peeled off the front of the van to reveal blackened metal underneath. Another fireman, after confirming I was the owner, asked what was in the back.

"Nothing," I replied, so quietly he had to ask me to repeat myself.

I felt numb inside as I stood there, wearing just the vest and underpants I'd gone to sleep in, staring at the burnt out shell of my van. Someone draped a blanket over me and I felt Marley's arm around my shoulder. He produced a flask of white rum and encouraged me to take a sip. It helped take away the taste and the smell of smoke and oil. I brushed the sweat from my brow and my damp forearm came away black with soot.

"I don't see how I can go on," I said to no one in particular.

"You got insurance, man?" Marley asked.

"Yes, but they'll probably take weeks to pay out and I bet I'll only get half what I paid for the van. I have deliveries to make tomorrow," I said, and then corrected myself as I realised what time it was. "Today! I mean!"

I bowed my head remembering that I'd declined the option of a hire vehicle because at the time it seemed too expensive for my budget. A false economy, I realised with hindsight.

A policeman came up to me and said, "The vehicle is safe now but please don't touch it. Our forensics team still have more work to do but I can tell you now it looks like this fire was started deliberately. We will need to take a statement from you later this morning."

Maybe he'd heard us talking about insurance because he looked at me as if I'd set fire to the van myself to make a fraudulent claim.

I was too exhausted to argue so I just turned my back on him until I heard him move away.

"Don't worry 'bout a thing man, as my namesake sang, I'll vouch for you. I know you were asleep because your snoring kept me awake all night."

"Did it, Marley?" I asked guiltily.

"Na, 'course not man, that's just what I'll tell de cops, OK?"

He looked a mess. His gold pyjamas were covered in soot. I shook him warmly by the hand and said, "thanks mate, you're a good'un!"

There was no point in going back to bed so I showered and sat in my armchair in the dark waiting for dawn and wondering what the coming day would bring. At 6am I rang the supervisor at the depot where I was supposed to be doing freelance deliveries. He was unsympathetic and merely asked why I couldn't just hire a van for the day. When I told him I had to wait in for the police he just hung up and I had the feeling I'd be getting no more work there.

Later two more police officers called and appeared to believe me when I said I had no idea who started the fire. I mentioned the two guys after my catalytic converter but they seemed to think that was hardly a motive to set the van alight. After a lot of form filling, they gave me a crime number for the insurance and admitted sadly that it was probably vandals and their likelihood of catching them was slim to zero.

It felt like the end of the line as far as my business was concerned. I'd been twice targeted by thieves, beaten up and now my van was a burnt out shell. If this was what being self-employed was going to be like you could keep it! I sat around for most of the day feeling unable to move and just stared at my four walls in despair. How was I going to help Ella through uni? Most of my redundancy money was already used and now I had no means of earning. I supposed I'd have to sign-on at the Job Centre tomorrow and start claiming job seekers allowance but I doubted that would even cover the rent on my flat.

My situation felt hopeless and with this thought uppermost in mind I reluctantly picked up the phone and dialled Leon Cooper's number.

CHAPTER ELEVEN

The part of Leon Cooper's organisation I joined operated from one of his large warehouses tucked behind an industrial estate off Penarth Road. I'd been told to report at nine o'clock the following Monday and ask for Gabriel Winsome, who turned out to be a short cheerful Cockney with a limp.

"Most important thing first," he chirped, "how d'yer like yer coffee?"

"Black, no sugar, please."

Winsome took a dirty mug that stood on a draining board in the kitchen and inspected the inside. Then he wiped the rim with his finger and swilled the mug under a cold tap before drying it on a grey tea towel that may have once been white. The black coffee had rainbow coloured bubbles floating on its surface and I resolved to bring my own mug tomorrow.

There were two desks in the room that looked like they'd been around since the 1950s. Winsome sat at one and invited me to sit opposite. He handed me what appeared to be a standard job contract, which I read quickly and signed.

"Yer now an official employee of Coopers Logistics

PLC," Winsome said, giving me a firm handshake. "Welcome to my world. After we've drunk the coffee I'll show yer 'round the depot. It'll be quiet out there at the moment coz most of the drivers are out delivering and the earliest won't be back until about four-ish."

His limp made him bob up and down when he walked. He leaned forward at a slight angle when he moved which, combined with the limp, made it seem as though his feet were constantly trying to keep up with the forward momentum of the rest of his body. I had to practically trot to keep up.

Winsome told me this was just one of forty similar depots around the country. I was impressed by the size of the operation and began to understand why Leon could afford such a large and luxurious house.

Before me were rows and rows of tiered shelves stretching into the distance with anonymous cartons and crates of all shapes and sizes. Winsome explained that barcode readers, he called them lasers, were used to track movement from the moment goods arrived to the moment they were delivered, so that if customers enquired they could be told immediately where their deliveries were in the chain.

Halfway down the length of the warehouse was another office with glass panels that overlooked the whole floor. Inside, five women and two men sat at computer screens with headsets connected to the phones. Winsome explained that most of them were dealing with orders or enquiries and said he'd take me to meet them later.

We encountered just a few men in overalls moving quietly between the aisles and whenever our paths crossed, Winsome introduced me as the new Special Deliveries Manager which was the first time I'd heard any mention of a job title.

"Like I said, the place is quiet now but early in the morning there's people trippin' over 'emselves. It's like a bleeding ants' nest!" Winsome said.

At the far end of the warehouse two massive doors opened onto a platform.

"This is 'Goods Inward' where the big trailers deliver all the stuff coming in," Winsome continued, acting as tour guide. "We've got a night shift comes in 'ere about eight o'clock to unload so everything's ready to go first thing in the morning."

"How many people are employed here?" I asked.

"It varies; during peaks we take on a lot of casuals but all told there's probably about fifteen full-timers on the payroll."

We rounded a corner and nearly collided with a tall, heavy-set man in overalls.

"Why don't you look where yer goin', yer bleeding great oaf!" Winsome yelled.

"Why don't you, Winnie, you've got eyes too!"

With that both of them burst out laughing and I hoped they hadn't noticed my own reaction. There was something about the way he was carrying the large spanner that made me recognise in an instant the man responsible for smashing up my van with a crowbar.

"This is the new special deliveries guy, Martin Blake," Winsome said.

If he noticed anything strange about the way I imagined I must look, he didn't say so. "Marty, this is Mike, the Mechanic. Anything needs servicing on yer van, this is yer man."

Yes, I've already been on the receiving end of one of his services, I thought, wondering how I should react. I stood rooted to the spot feeling mildly sick as Mike swapped the spanner from his right to his left hand and rubbed his right hand clean on his overalls before offering it to me.

"Leon told me you'd be starting today. It's good to meet you, Marty," he said, not showing a flicker of recognition, although I had the distinct feeling this Mike knew precisely who I was and where we'd met before.

Maintaining eye contact, I took the massive proffered hand and felt some pain as my fingers were briefly gripped in a vice and then released.

"Actually, it's Martin, not Marty," I said.

There was an awkward silence and then the mechanic excused himself and moved off in the direction of the office.

Winsome looked at the man's receding back and then turned thoughtfully to me but whatever he was thinking he kept to himself.

"That about concludes the tour," he said, "let's go and meet the enquiries team on our way back."

I followed him, quietly wondering what, if anything, I should do or say about Mike. It confirmed to me that Leon may have had more of a part in the whole thing than he was letting on. Perhaps they all knew what had happened but were deliberately choosing to ignore it and move on. Besides, what was there to discuss; it had happened, I'd been generously recompensed. I sensed that for Mike at least it had been nothing personal and as for the other guy in the baseball cap... Not for the first time, I felt curious about his fate but suspected I may never get to the bottom of it, and it was probably better that way.

Winsome opened the door to the office with a flourish and, ignoring the fact that at least five of the people in the room were on the phone, announced loudly, "This is Marty, our new specials guy everyone!" I winced at the shortening of my name but didn't try and correct him. Clearly, Winsome didn't intend to introduce each of them by name, perhaps because he didn't know all their names himself. The three not on the phone gathered around and introduced themselves as Clive, Jan and Cathy. Those on the phone just nodded at me and smiled almost apologetically. One of the women seemed to be having a particularly trying conversation with a difficult customer and I was impressed with the way she was handling it.

We left them and began walking back to our own office

after Winsome declared all this talking had left him in dire
need of another cuppa.

The woman who'd been on the phone came running
after us, calling, "Winnie, that was Harry Rodgers on the
phone demanding his parcel is delivered this afternoon.
Have we got anyone who can do it?" she asked, looking
speculatively at me.

"Looks like you've got your first job, Marty" Winsome
said.

I turned to follow the woman but Winsome grabbed
my arm and said, "Come and 'ave a cuppa first though!"

*

Later, Winsome handed me a bunch of keys and a log
book and said, "These are for yer new van, Marty."

I was shocked to see my name already filled in as the
new owner.

"We prefer to employ owner-drivers," he explained,
"it's better for tax reasons."

"That's very generous," I said, lost for words.

"We ain't that kind; we'll be docking monthly payments
from yer wages until it's all paid for. Now go an' get that
parcel."

I collected the package for Harry Rodgers from the
woman, whose name turned out to be Debbie. She told
me that Mr Rodgers was an important customer but could
be difficult at times. I was told to be sure to get a signature
for the receipt of the package. The package itself was no
bigger than a shoe box but extremely heavy for its size.
There was nothing on the label to indicate what was inside.
I wondered what could be so important.

The address was in a village I'd never heard of called
Coed Manor, somewhere between Cowbridge and Llantwit
Major in the Vale of Glamorgan. According to my satnav
the round trip would take up the best part of the
afternoon. Winsome told me I'd needn't come back
afterwards and that he'd see me same time tomorrow
morning. I was relieved to learn I wasn't expected to arrive

with the dawn chorus of early starters and assumed their intention was to break me in gradually.

Coed Manor was a sleepy little hamlet in the middle of nowhere and I wondered if I could rely on the satnav not to take me down roads unsuitable for this brand new van. At one particularly narrow stretch with grass growing in the middle of the road, I met someone in a Bentley coming the other way and had to reverse several hundred yards to a passing place. The driver didn't even acknowledge me. It irked me even more when I discovered that the stuck-up git had just passed a suitable spot about twenty feet back!

The houses were all large and most had extensive grounds and it took me another fifteen minutes to find the right address as there wasn't a soul around to ask.

I had no idea who Harry Rodgers was but felt sure he would be on the high net worth list of clients wherever he banked. The house was even bigger than Leon's place, and I spotted a tennis court and a swimming pool tucked discreetly to one side of the property.

The entrance was grand with a large gravel drive and a beautifully planted traffic island in the middle.

I rang the bell and was surprised when a portly old man in a torn string vest, puffing a cigar, opened the door.

"Mr Rodgers?" I asked.

"Who wants to know?" the man demanded blowing smoke in my face and then he saw the package and added, "about bloody time too!"

He snatched the heavy box out of my hands and slammed the door without another word.

Nonplussed, I leaned on the doorbell until he returned.

"What now?" he said, glaring at me.

"I need a signature," I said, indicating the electronic gadget that Debbie had thrust in my hand as I'd left the depot.

The man looked down at the parcel in his fat hands and then back at me and said, "Fuck off!"

This time the door slammed so hard the knocker

jangled.

I decided to give up and retreat as I wasn't sure what the man might be capable of if I dared to disturb him again. I scribbled the word 'delivered' on the signature line of the gadget and climbed back in the van. Sod it.

I had no way of knowing that the next time I encountered Harry Rodgers he would be a corpse.

CHAPTER TWELVE

I was back in time to grab a quick coffee at Beth's Café before closing time. There were a few lone people sitting at scattered tables but it was pretty quiet. It was a beautiful sunny day and people were probably favouring cold drinks outside.

Beth seemed pleased to see me, and when I mentioned I had a job her eyes lit up and she said she'd bring my coffee over and I could tell her all about it. I found a nice quiet table in a corner at the back of the cafe.

"Congratulations!" Beth said, bringing my coffee and one for herself. "I thought it wouldn't be long before someone snapped you up. A man with your talent is wasted driving a van. I suppose this means I'll have to find a new delivery man now though."

"No you won't, because I'm still a van driver," I said, "and my new boss is very flexible about what hours I do and said I could carry on with some of my clients as long as the work doesn't clash with his."

"Well, that's very generous of him but what if it does clash? What am I supposed to do for a driver then?"

"I must admit, I hadn't really thought of that. But this man I work for has plenty of drivers at his disposal so I'm sure we could work something out."

Beth looked uncertain. "And who is 'this man' you work for?"

"A chap called Leon Cooper, have you heard of him?"

She turned a shade paler.

"Oh Martin, everyone has heard of him. Are you sure you want to become involved with someone like that? Did you know the driver who beat you up used to work for him?"

"Well, not until Leon told me he'd sacked him when he heard what he'd done to me and he paid me compensation for the damage and offered me this job. Sure he bends the rules sometimes but I don't believe he'd harm anybody."

Beth looked as though she was about to argue, but a customer came into the cafe and she had to go and serve him.

While I was finishing my coffee, my mobile rang. It was Detective Sergeant Bryn Williams wanting to know if I could call into the station any time soon.

*

Twenty minutes later, I was sitting opposite Williams. During the short drive to the station I'd been thinking what I might say following my new-found alliance with Leon Cooper. To all intents and purposes, in my mind, the case was resolved and I wasn't sure how wise it would be to pursue it any further through the police.

We were soon joined by a Detective Inspector who Williams introduced as Bruno Cannard. He had a world-weary look in his eyes and tiny red veins in his nose which suggested a fondness for alcohol.

"In your statement," Cannard said, so quietly that I had to lean forward and concentrate to hear him," you say that you were summoned to this remote place by a telephone caller. Is that correct?"

"Yes. It sounded like an elderly man on the other end of the line."

"You may not be aware, Mr Blake, that after you were

attacked, a member of the public phoned in to alert the emergency services. We would like you to listen to this recording of the 999 call made advising us of your situation."

Cannard spoke slowly. He reached out a nicotine-stained finger and pressed a button that brought his laptop back to life and clicked on the play button.

The quality of the digital recording was very good and I listened to a voice saying, "There's a bloke at these coordinates needs yer 'elp."

He repeated the coordinates again and then hung up, ignoring the operator's request for his name and number.

There was something vaguely familiar about the tone and accent of the voice that reminded me of Gabriel Winsome maybe trying to disguise his voice through a cloth.

After a short silence, Cannard said, "Is that the same voice that arranged the collection?"

"Can I hear it again please?" I asked, more to buy thinking time rather than from any need to listen again.

Cannard clicked play and once more the voice filled the room. I still couldn't be absolutely certain that it was Winsome but it wouldn't surprise me if it were his voice. But then I'd already decided not to give them anything more.

"I'm not sure," I said. "The voices were similar but it was a long time ago and a lot has happened since I received that first call."

Cannard looked at me incredulously. "I would have thought it was quite a distinctive voice and not one that you could easily forget."

"Well I'm sorry but there's no way I could say with any confidence in court that those voices were anything other than similar."

"Sergeant Williams here tells me you think you recognised the men who assaulted you when you were going through our known offenders' album."

I looked again at the photographs of the men I now knew to be Mike the mechanic at Coopers Logistics and the man in the red baseball cap. I pretended to study their pictures again, and after what I thought was a suitable length of time said, "Now that I see them again, I don't think these were the men. I didn't get a good look at them."

Cannard sighed.

"If these are not the men, then why did you pick them out in the first place?" He sounded exasperated.

I pursed my lips. "I'm not sure, maybe I was just trying too hard to help find the people that did this, and maybe I was just a bit over eager because, looking at them again now, I'm no longer sure."

Cannard and Williams exchanged frustrated glances and then Cannard closed the file and said, "That will be all for now, thank you Mr Blake. I am sorry to say we have made no progress in finding the men and have precious little to go on.

"Naturally we will keep trying and if anything develops we shall be in touch. Meanwhile, if you remember anything else about the incident that you would like to discuss with me you'll find my number on this card. If I am unavailable, please leave a message."

*

Back in the flat, I felt at a loose end as the evening loomed. I hated having no one to talk to and found myself missing my wife and daughter and wondering what they were doing. I picked up the mobile and pressed the speed dial button for Ella. She always took an age to answer her phone and never used the voicemail service. I'd asked her why not on one occasion and she explained to me that if people call her they're paying for the call, whereas if they leave a message they expect her to ring back and then she's paying for the call. So although I found it frustrating when I couldn't reach her, I couldn't help but admire her thriftiness. It boded well for her immediate future as a cash-starved student.

I was just about to give up when she answered.

"Hi Dad, how you doing?" she said. "I was going to ring you later!"

She always said that and it always made me smile. It was lovely and also heartbreaking to hear her voice again – my little girl was growing up fast and I couldn't help feeling I was losing her. Even before all this blew up with Katrina I'd been fighting to come to terms with her leaving for uni.

"I'm doing fine thanks. How are you, my lovely?"

"I'm cool."

"And what about your Mum, is she okay?"

Ella hesitated, then said, "She's okay I guess."

Ella sounded to me like she felt it was awkward talking to me about her mother so I quickly changed the subject and said, "How about you and me going to the Juboraj for a bite to eat tomorrow?" It was her favourite Indian restaurant.

Again she hesitated before answering, "Er..., the thing is Dad, I've arranged to go to the cinema with the girls tomorrow night to see the new Robert Pattinson film before we go on holiday."

I'd forgotten she was off to France with her friends next week; the holiday had been booked after a difficult discussion between me and Katrina about whether she was responsible enough to go to France with her friends. Katrina said she was, but I wasn't convinced. Then Ella pointed out she was eighteen and didn't need my permission – the argument was abruptly ended.

"I know that, lovely," I said, trying to recover the situation, "that's why I wanted to meet you, so I could give you some holiday spending cash. Why don't we meet early, say about six o'clock, and then you can still go to the cinema with your friends afterwards?"

Suddenly, she seemed a lot more enthusiastic and readily agreed to meet.

*

Next morning, at the warehouse, Gabriel Winsome had placed a cup of black, instant coffee in front of me before I'd even got my coat off.

"Did you find that place ok yesterday?" Winsome asked.

"Yes, I did but the stroppy bloke who answered the door refused to sign for the parcel. When I asked he just told me to eff off!"

Winsome shrugged his shoulders. "Some people ain't got no manners," he said disparagingly.

A dark blue Jaguar pulled into the parking space in front of the office.

"Eh up," Winsome said, "'ere's the boss!"

Leon Cooper waited for his driver to get out and open the rear door of the car before emerging into the sunlight. He looked every inch the Chief Executive of a large organisation, wearing a tailored pin-stripe suit, powdery blue shirt with a white collar and a silk tie with a gold thread running through it. To round it off a matching silk handkerchief graced his breast pocket.

He breezed confidently into the office and said, "Just thought I'd drop by and see how the new boy is doing!"

Winsome jumped up and made him a coffee.

We'd just settled down when Debbie from the office approached the glass door, knocked and then discreetly waited outside until Winsome gave her the nod.

She poked her head shyly around the door, smiled and said "Good morning Mr Cooper," and then looked pointedly at me before asking, "Could I have a quick word with Mr Winsome, please?"

Winsome looked irritated but Leon waved him away, adding, "It's ok Gabe, it's Martin I wanted to chat to. We'll catch up later."

When they'd gone he turned to me and said, "Have you heard any more from the police about the attack on you?"

Did he know that I'd been called back to the police

station yesterday? I decided it would be safer not to lie to him.

"They asked me to pop into the station yesterday to listen to a recording of the 999 call. It sounded like the same person who lured me out there in the first place." I chose not to mention that the voice sounded a like Winsome putting on an 'old' voice.

Leon looked at me for a second and said, "Did you recognise the voice?"

"No, it sounded like an old man, could've been anyone..."

Leon waited.

"There was something else," I began, cautiously. "The first time I went there, they asked me to look through their mugshot album and I picked out the guy in the baseball cap that you say worked for you."

I hesitated before continuing. "There was also a picture of Mike and although I was less sure about it I told them at the time I thought he *may* have been the other one.

Leon frowned at this piece of news.

"Last night I met an Inspector Cannard who seemed to be very interested in them and asked me to take another look at the photos to see if I could be any more certain."

The flicker of a smile played at the corner of Leon's mouth. "Ah, my old friend Inspector Duck."

I must've looked at him blankly because he added, "He doesn't spell it correctly but Canard with one 'n' is French for duck – and what did you tell Monsieur Duck, Martin?"

"I said that, on reflection, I didn't recognise either of them as the men who attacked me. I told them the one who looked like Mike was fairer and possibly a bit smaller in build."

Leon nodded. "You did well under the circumstances. Thank you for keeping Mike out of it – he was only acting on instructions. It was nothing personal, just business, you know that now don't you?"

I nodded.

"Did you tell them you've since met Mike?" Leon shook his head. "Daft question, of course you didn't."

"They didn't ask and I didn't say."

Leon looked thoughtful.

"That explains why they were watching the place yesterday afternoon and Mike says he was followed home by two plain-clothes."

He paused, clearly deep in thought. "It wouldn't be good if they made a connection between you and Mike as that would be bound to raise their curiosity. Presumably they don't know you're working for me yet and it would probably be better to keep it that way. I'll get Gabriel to set you up with a laptop and a mobile phone and you can work from home for the time being. Thanks for being so honest with me, Martin."

I felt relieved, as though I'd just passed some kind of test.

Winsome returned. "Harry Rodgers is up to his old tricks!" he said as he came through the door.

"What's that damned man done now?" Leon asked.

"His parcel got pulled out of line and delayed by our suspicious parcels procedure," Winsome explained, "and Rodgers got on the phone really pissed that he hadn't received it so we sent Marty up there, special delivery, yesterday. He refused to sign for it and now the bastard's saying he still hasn't received it!"

"I'm sure I took it to the right place," I chipped in, "it took me ages to find it but the number was clearly marked on the property and he was obviously expecting me because when he took the parcel he said, 'about bloody time'."

"There's no doubt in my mind you were in the right place, Martin," Leon reassured him. "This is not the first time he's tried it on with us. The trouble is the man's a crook, but a pretty big player and we felt it would be less trouble in the long run to work with him rather than not. But I'm not sure that's true anymore. He's being a right pain in the arse and trying to put muscle on local businesses wherever he can.

"Do we know what was in the package, Gabriel?"

Winsome moved very close to Leon and whispered something in his ear that I didn't catch.

"No wonder he didn't want to sign for it then!" Leon's eyes sparkled as he looked at me. "At least it proves our suspicious packages routine works."

Leon's eyes never left my face. "There should be no secrets between the three of us from now on," he said. "It seems that Harry Rodgers has turned you into an unwitting gun runner, Martin. The package contained an automatic pistol."

I felt my stomach cramping and bile rising in his throat. I thrust my hands into my trouser pockets to stop them shaking.

"But if we knew what the package contained," I uttered, still in shock, "why did we still deliver it instead of..."

"...going to the police? That's a good question Martin, but, as I already explained to you, we accepted that working with Rodgers was the lesser of two evils. He would make a powerful enemy! And, besides, the last thing we want is a warehouse crawling with coppers like wasps around a nest. Who knows what else they might stumble across?"

"How we gonna handle this, Boss?" Winsome asked.

"Leave it with me," Leon said. "I'll speak to Rodgers and sort this out. Meanwhile Gabriel, I want you to set Martin up to work from home. We know the police are stalking Mike at the moment and it may prove useful to have someone on the team with no known association with us."

That sounded ominous to me but I remained silent.

Winsome and I watched as Leon's driver stood to attention and held open the rear door of the Jaguar for Leon to embark like royalty.

"He's an incredible geezer!" Winsome declared, with a look of pure hero-worship.

CHAPTER THIRTEEN

Winsome sent Mike the mechanic outside to check there were no policemen lurking in doorways or parked cars. The coast was clear so I was sent home armed with a laptop, some kind of security dongle, and a new mobile phone. Winsome told me in no uncertain terms that I must only use this equipment for business purposes, and that the phone had only three pre-programmed numbers stored on it and was untraceable. The numbers were for himself, Leon and Mike, and were similarly untraceable to themselves. It was clear that Coopers Logistics took security very seriously.

I was beginning to fear I'd made a mistake taking this job as I snuck out of the warehouse like a schoolboy playing truant from school. All the way back to the flat I kept checking my wing mirrors to see if anyone was following me. At one point I saw a red saloon car on my tail and deliberately turned into a street I didn't want to go down. The red car also turned completely unnerving me. I found myself in a cul-de-sac with nowhere to go and when I turned around I saw that the driver was a young woman with a child in a car seat who gave me a puzzled look as she pulled into her drive. I was becoming ridiculously paranoid.

When I finally made it back to my flat, I collapsed into a chair exhausted. I could scarcely believe that yesterday afternoon I'd delivered a gun to some kind of underworld gangster. What if I'd rung the bell a third time and insisted on that signature? Would the bloke have shot me with the gun I'd just delivered? What a bloody mess!

I remembered the last thing that Leon said to me when he offered me the job was that some of his interests fell slightly outside of the law. He gave me one last opportunity to accept the job and all that came with it, or walk away. Looking back on that moment, I remembered guiltily the buzz of excitement that coursed through me which, coupled with the generous salary, had made the decision seem easy. But now I felt taken aback by the speed at which I'd been drawn into a world of guns and lying to the police.

I spent an hour or so setting up the new laptop then switched it off and wondered if I should hide the damn thing under the floorboards, or somewhere similar, before telling myself to stop being so melodramatic.

I showered and changed and went to the post office to convert some cash into Euros for Ella to take on holiday. At least now, I could afford to be generous.

*

I noticed a woman in a very tight, short skirt standing outside the Indian restaurant and was a bit shocked to see it was my little Ella. And was that a cigarette stub she hastily dropped as I approached? She greeted me with a squeal of delight and a big hug. Immediately, I could smell the smoke on her clothes but this wasn't the time or place to have a fight about it. I wished she didn't have to rush off so soon afterwards to a movie. We ordered a meal and I noticed that the waiter could scarcely take his eyes off Ella. I felt a mix of fatherly pride and concern for her virtue. Once again, I was struck by her beauty and wondered when exactly she'd transformed into such a glamorous woman.

I listened carefully as she recited their holiday plans, trying not to let my concern show on my face. They were planning to tour southern France visiting vineyards and staying in gites with six of her friends from school, all of whom had successfully passed their exams and were going on to their various universities. I'd met some of the girls and they seemed a pretty sensible bunch and I suppose there'd be safety in numbers. I was also impressed that Ella seemed to be the one doing all the organising and wondered how much input, if any, Katrina had had in the selection of the accommodation.

I felt I was doing well but in the end I couldn't resist giving the usual father/daughter lecture on the perils of getting drunk in nightclubs and the predatory boys that hung around these places.

"But Dad," Ella protested, "the whole point of the holiday is to get drunk and lose our virginity to as many boys as we can!"

I stared at her open-mouthed and speechless!

She giggled, and said, "Ha ha! You should see your face Dad! You really don't have to worry. I promise I'm not going to get gang-banged or pregnant; we're just going out there to have a good time and party. Trust me!"

I took her hands in mine and looked into her eyes, "I do trust you Ella and I want you to have fun!"

I made a show of tapping my jacket pockets and then pulled out the envelope containing €300. "This should help," I said, handing it to her. "Don't spend it all on the first night!"

"Wow Dad!" she gasped. "This is amazing; are you sure you want to give me all this?"

"Of course I'm sure. The business is doing a little better now and you deserve it for working so hard and passing exams."

Ella beamed at me and I studied her face trying to capture every detail in it, those blue trusting eyes, the cute little nose that turned up slightly at the tip, just like her mother's. I just wanted to hold this moment and cherish it in my memory forever.

*

The following morning I had a delivery to do for Beth and she took up immediately where our last conversation had ended.

"So what's this job with Leon Cooper entail exactly?" she demanded.

She looked genuinely concerned.

"Did you know the driver you used before me worked for Leon?"

Beth looked thoughtful, "Certainly not," she said, "but it doesn't really surprise me. I suppose it explains a lot actually!"

I must've raised my eyebrows, because she carried on quickly. "I've heard things about Leon Cooper, Martin, things that have made me want to steer well clear of him and men like him."

"Things like what?"

Beth wouldn't be drawn on what she'd heard, insisting that she wasn't a gossip. I tried my best to persuade her to tell me but she steadfastly refused.

All she would add was, "He has a reputation for being a dangerous and ruthless man capable of doing whatever it takes to get his way. Reputation is everything when you're in business for yourself and you would do well to remember that, Martin. Especially when you're just starting out. All I'm saying is you don't want to get your own reputation tarnished by association with the likes of him!"

I'd intended to tell her more about how Leon had come to pay for the repairs and offer me the job but now I thought better of it. In any case, Leon's warning about discussing his business with others rang in my ears.

In the end I just said, "Does this mean you'd prefer not to use me for your deliveries anymore?"

Her expression softened a little, "Of course not. I

know you're trustworthy and reliable and would never knowingly let me down. It's just that I'm concerned that you may not know what you're getting into. Be careful, Martin, that's all I ask."

"I will," I promised.

I felt genuinely touched. I reckoned she was probably about ten years younger than me and yet in so many ways she seemed older and wiser. She'd been in charge of the cafe for a long time now and had turned it from a greasy spoon into a decent coffee shop. It could sometimes be hot in the kitchen so she didn't bother with a lot of make-up and always wore a clean pair of overalls under a starched-white apron. I tried to imagine her in a dress with her hair done and thought she'd look pretty damn good. It struck me then that although I'd often talked to her about myself and my family I knew practically nothing about her. I didn't even know if she had a partner, or a family, although I'd always assumed she had. I was glad that she was still willing for me to continue with her deliveries. It felt like a vote of confidence.

After completing her delivery, I had nothing much else to do that day so I returned to the flat and checked my new laptop for any emails. There were a couple of general circulation-type emails in the inbox but nothing specifically addressed to me. I was glad it was Friday and the weekend was approaching. It had been a strange first week and I still didn't have a clear picture of what my role in Coopers Logistics was exactly. The environment was so alien to what I'd been used to in the bank, where I'd had a clear job description, induction courses, on-the-job training and so on. There'd been none of that and Leon seemed content to pay me to sit around at home and do nothing.

I flopped into an armchair and thought about Beth's warning, wondering again what I was getting myself into and how things might pan out when my new mobile phone rang. The ringtone startled me because I'd never heard it before and for a couple of seconds wondered what was making the noise. It was Winsome. "We've gotta job for yer tomorrow night." he said.

"But tomorrow's Saturday," I protested.

"No shit!"

"Sorry," I backtracked, "that's not a problem, Leon did explain about flexibility, I'm just not used to working weekends."

"Well you're gonna have to get used to it mate, you're not a banker anymore you know." He put on his posh voice and added, "Sorry if we're disrupting your plans, old chap!"

"I didn't have any plans," I said, without rising to the bait.

"Good, I want you to pick Mike and me up in yer van from the car park at the Old Dragon Inn at eleven-thirty tomorrow night. You know where that is?"

"Yes, it's in Canton isn't it? Eleven thirty at night?"

"Correct. Don't be late."

CHAPTER FOURTEEN

The next evening at eleven fifteen, as I expected, the Old Dragon was beginning to tip its drunks out onto the street. A few people were getting into cars to drive home but most were hailing cabs or weaving off unsteadily for the walk home. There were plenty of spaces in the car park. There was no sign of Winsome or Mike and I assumed they'd probably be inside. I wondered irritably if this was just some sort of wind-up to get me to meet and drive them home after they'd had a few drinks.

I sat tapping the steering wheel impatiently watching the hands on the dashboard clock move slowly towards half past eleven. It was a mild night and I had the window down so heard Winsome's throaty laughter before actually spotting them. I don't know why but it felt like they were laughing at my expense. What did surprise me was that they'd come from a different direction than the pub and so hadn't been inside after all.

Winsome opened the passenger-side door and climbed in with Mike following just behind him. The cab could comfortably seat three people.

"If it isn't Marty the banker!" Winsome declared, slapping me on the back.

I'd given up insisting my name was Martin and not Marty but this was the first time I'd heard 'the banker' tagged onto the end. Maybe he gave some sort of qualifier to all his acquaintances, like he called Mike 'Mike the mechanic'. I supposed it could've been worse and in a strange way it felt like a form of acceptance that I was becoming one of them.

Winsome became more serious and the mood in the van changed. "Turn left out of the car park and then take the first right," he said.

"Where are we going?"

"You'll see. Now take the next left."

I followed instructions until we arrived at the next junction where I just stopped.

"What you stop for?" Winsome demanded.

"I'm waiting for your directions," I replied sarcastically.

Winsome muttered an apology. "Left."

We travelled a few miles and came to a large council estate where some seventies architect designed it so that all the houses fronted onto a green area leaving vehicular access to the rear. The houses were mostly terraced or 'linked' and occupants had to walk a small distance from their door to a courtyard of garages that doubled as a football pitch for the kids during the day. Someone had drawn a goal post on a wall and a crude effigy had been drawn hanging from it with a noose around its neck.

Winsome indicated a grubby garage door that had once been white but was now a grey/green mix of grime and moss. "Back up to that one and park as close as you can. Leave just enough room for us to open the door."

I did as he asked. Mike jumped out and went towards the garage doors jangling keys, and Winsome walked around to the back of the van and opened the rear doors.

"What the fuck?" he exclaimed.

I felt sheepish. "I've been emptying my garage and didn't make it to the tip in time."

"Look at this, Mike," Winsome called irritably. "Will we

still get our stuff in 'ere?"

Mike cocked his head to one side. "It'll be a tight squeeze."

Winsome turned to me and said, "Next time we call you to a job, make sure the bloody van is empty! OK?"

"Will do."

"Well don't just stand there, come and 'elp us load these boxes."

Reluctantly I climbed out of the cab. The boxes were about the size of bedside tables and quite heavy to lift. Thankfully, to my relief, there was sufficient room in the back of the van. There were no labels or anything else on the boxes to indicate what they might contain. I surreptitiously shook one as I carried it but there was nothing loose inside to give the contents away. After my last 'special delivery' I took some comfort that the boxes weren't heavy enough to be packed with guns.

All the same, the fact that the boxes were being transported at the dead of night in such a clandestine way had my nerves on edge and I could feel my left eyelid jumping with some kind of nervous tick. I hope the others wouldn't notice.

When all the boxes were packed Winsome told me to go and start the van while he and Mike disappeared back into the garage. When they came back out Winsome walked around to the front of the van and bent down as if he were tying his shoe laces. He was carrying something but I couldn't make out what. Meanwhile, I heard Mike at the back of the van checking the rear doors were properly shut. Both men climbed into the passenger seats beside me and I baulked when saw they were each carrying pistols.

"Oh Jesus Christ! What the hell are they for?"

"Insurance," Mike replied calmly; it was one of the few things he'd said all night.

"I don't want any part of this!" I yelled.

"Don't be an idiot," Winsome snapped, his voice rising in anger. "Just shut up and drive."

I switched off the engine and took the keys out of the ignition.

"What do you think you're doing now?" Winsome said.

Mike just sat calmly waiting with watchful eyes that flicked from face-to-face constantly assessing the situation. I wondered if maybe he was ex-military, SAS even; he was certainly big enough and calm in a crisis.

"I'm not moving until you tell me where we're going and why we need the guns," I insisted.

Winsome remained silent, holding my stare. He looked dangerous and I wondered for a second if he was about to threaten me with the gun. I swallowed at the thought, knowing I'd have no chance of escape at such close quarters.

Something seemed to click in Winsome's face like he'd reached a decision.

"OK," he said, exhaling slowly, "we're going to do a cash deal and deliver this stuff to some business acquaintances of Leon's. We've done business with them before but we're not a hundred percent certain we can trust them to pay. The guns are purely there to dissuade them from any funny business. The chances are they'll be tooled up as well for the same reasons as us. So like Mike said, they're just insurance. We ain't never 'ad to use 'em yet, eh Mike?"

Mike, the man of few words, shook his head.

"And what's in the boxes?" I wanted to know. "Guns? Drugs? Stolen goods?"

Winsome said, "Trust me, Marty, it's better you don't know!"

"I want to know what I'm getting into."

"It's not guns, and Leon doesn't ever deal in drugs. He went so ape once when someone gave his daughter some bad ecstasy – he went back and torched the club."

I vaguely remembered a nightclub being burned to the ground a couple of years back. Our bank had appointed an insurance investigator when we discovered it was arson.

"So is it stolen goods then?"

"Truth is, Marty, we don't know what it is ourselves yet. It gives a certain amount of 'deniability' if the cops pick us up. We'll probably find out when our associates open the boxes to check it's what they're expecting."

"And if it isn't?"

Winsome tapped the gun on his lap. "Insurance," he said. "Now are you gonna start this bloody van? We don't want to piss these people off by being late!"

"I'm not happy about this," I said, restarting the engine.

"Tough shit!" Winsome snapped. "Leon warned you, some of his transactions weren't always kosher. Why do you think he's paying you double the rate of most of our depot drivers? It ain't benevolence, let me tell you!"

"He never said anything about carrying guns!" I muttered, pulling away.

"You ain't carrying, we are," Winsome said, "so stop bloody moaning."

The rendezvous area was a cleared patch of ground in the middle of an industrial estate that bordered the docks area of the city. The place looked deserted but Winsome told me to drive all the way around the perimeter to check for any signs of surveillance. I thought they really had picked a good spot because there was very little cover of any description in which an observer might hide. There were also several access roads down which they could escape if the need arose. I couldn't even believe I was thinking this way. Been watching too many movies, I thought as, despite the knots in my stomach and my anger at the situation, there was a tiny inner core somewhere deep inside of me that found the whole operation exciting. I felt a heady mix of fear, anticipation and adrenalin, until Winsome brought me back to reality.

"Now then, Marty; whatever goes down here you're not under any circumstances to get out of the van. You stay in your seat and keep the engine running. Like I said to you, we ain't expecting any trouble but if they do come on to us

I want you to hightail it out of here. You got that?"

I nodded, "What about you and Mike?"

"Don't you worry about us, we can 'andle ourselves. The most important thing for you to remember is that you've got high value merchandise in the back of this van and Leon will expect you to protect his investment. OK?

"You drive far away and park up somewhere safe, don't go 'ome, just lay low, and stay with the van and guard the goods until someone calls the mobile I gave yer."

I took the phone from my pocket and checked it was switched on.

"Right, take the van into the middle ground and we'll sit and wait," Winsome said, glancing at his watch. "They should be 'ere any minute."

Five minutes later a dark coloured van appeared and drove in a slow circuit around the site. I guessed they were checking for surveillance in much the same way as we had a few minutes earlier. The three of us watched in silence as the van pulled off the road and stopped in front of us. When the driver killed the headlights it left us temporarily blinded in the sudden darkness.

There was a moment of stillness while we all sat in silence, like gunfighters waiting to see who made the first move. We waited some more until our eyes readjusted to the darkness. It was cloudy so there was no moon but some amber light filtered across from the few surrounding street lights that still had intact bulbs.

Two men got out of the van and started walking towards us, one carrying a briefcase.

Mike opened his door and stepped out quickly followed by Winsome who whispered urgently to me, "Remember, first sign of trouble and you drive away as fast as you can and if these guys try to follow you, make sure you lose them!"

I watched them tucking their guns into the back of their belts as they walked away with their backs to me.

The four men met in the middle of no man's land and I could hear low murmuring voices but couldn't tell what was being said. I watched as the man with the briefcase opened the lid and held it up for Mike to inspect the contents. He took what looked like a wad of bank notes out and fanned them. Then he shook his head, threw the wad back into the briefcase and pushed the man violently away. The man tripped and fell backwards. Voices were raised and the other man threw a punch at Winsome who dodged it like a seasoned boxer and threw one of his own. It was enough to send his assailant to the ground and Winsome glanced over his shoulder and waved frantically at me to get going. That cost him vital seconds, allowing the man on the floor to lash out with his feet causing Winsome to double up. Mike and the other man were still grappling together on the ground.

I felt the sweat trickling down my spine and gathering in the small of his back. My knuckles were white on the steering wheel as I watched the fight unfolding, paralysed with fear, torn between jumping out to help and just following instructions.

All four were wrestling on the ground now but both Mike and Winsome appeared to be on top.

Something finally snapped in my brain as my fight or flight response kicked in. I opted for flight, as instructed, and thrust the van into first gear. I let the clutch out too quickly. The van stalled and I cursed, frantically turning the key to restart it. After a cough and splutter, the engine sprang back into life and I sped over the bumpy ground, hoping whatever I was carrying in the back wasn't fragile. Finally, I reach the road and smooth tarmac.

I turned right along the perimeter of the open ground and watched helplessly as two men broke away from the others and ran towards the other van. I couldn't tell from this distance whether the two were Mike and Winsome or the other guys but whoever they were they'd got in the van and it was coming after me!

"...if they follow, make sure you lose them!" Winsome's words echoed in my mind. I floored the accelerator, the perspiration still running down my back felt like it was turning to ice.

I had a minute or so start on the other van so I kept my speed to the most I felt I could safely handle and just prayed that I wouldn't turn the van over or, worse, run into a police patrol and get stopped for speeding.

On reaching the main roads I was surprised by how much traffic was still about in the early hours of Sunday morning. It seemed every other car was a taxi, presumably ferrying people home from the nightclubs. Apart from the occasional bank Christmas do, this was a world I hadn't frequented for the best part of thirty years and I was way out of my comfort zone. I checked the wing mirrors for any sign of the other van following but saw nothing. Easing up on the speed a little in the traffic I thought I must've lost the other van – maybe it wasn't even trying to chase me. Maybe they were just as keen to get away from the scene as I was. I felt a bit safer on the main road with more people were around and my heart slowed a little.

I wondered what had happened to Winsome and Mike. Were they ok? What if they'd been left for dead on that patch of waste ground? Should I turn back and check? What was it Winsome had told me to do? Find somewhere out of the way and lay low until they rang the mobile. I looked at the phone sitting next to me on the passenger seat and willed it to light up with a call but it remained stubbornly dark and silent.

Then I heard a siren getting nearer and spotted a blue light flashing in my wing mirrors, steadily gaining on me. Oh shit! What now? Should I pull over, or try and escape? My heart was threatening to burst through my chest. I quickly realised that I hadn't a hope of outrunning, or losing, the police car in the van so I pulled over to the side of the road and waited for the blue lights to catch me up. While waiting, I frantically tried to concoct some plausible story in my head to explain what I was doing out in a van at this time of night. I needn't have worried as they sped past me without so much as a sideways glance.

I let out a long sigh of relief. My hands shook as I placed them back on the wheel and suddenly I felt engulfed by tiredness as the prolonged adrenalin rush began wearing off. I wasn't really safe to drive in such a state and tried to think where I might hide out. I remembered a lonely lay-by out near the reservoir where I used to take Katrina when we were courting many, many years ago and headed out that way.

There were just two other cars in the lay-by and both had steamed up windows. I parked as far away from them as I possibly could in a quiet dark corner and switched off the engine.

For a long time, I sat in the dark watching the orange lights from the city reflecting in the water and thought long and hard about the mess I was in. Just a short time ago I was in a safe and, I thought, secure job with a wife and daughter and a nice house in a decent part of town. How could I possibly have foreseen any of this coming? I remembered an album track from an old album by The Police with Sting's dulcet tones singing about how 'life was easy when it was boring'. How I wished I could go back to that old, boring life.

I picked up the mobile phone that Winsome had given me and checked again it was on and that there were no missed calls. Nothing. I had a feeling it was not going to ring tonight. I switched the radio on and listened to some late night music; my last memory was hearing Lou Reed's 'Walk On The Wild Side' before I must have drifted into an uneasy sleep where I dreamed I was being chased around the city by men with guns who were intent on killing me for whatever it was I had in the back.

Robert Darke

CHAPTER FIFTEEN

I awoke to ducks and geese squawking raucously across the reservoir. Cold, stiff and aching, my throat was dry and my teeth felt furry. It was six o'clock and the sun was already up. There was no sign of the other cars that had been there when I fell asleep and I hadn't heard them drive off. As I looked around a jeep pulling a hotdog trailer drove in and a man and woman got out and busied themselves setting up their pitch.

I wondered what business they thought they might possibly do this early on a Sunday morning in such a remote place. A few fishermen arrived and began setting up their rods. Soon they were ordering coffee and breakfast rolls and quite a queue formed waiting to be served. Maybe I'd gone into the wrong business.

The smell of cooking bacon was making me hungry but I didn't want to draw attention to myself, or have to explain why I was there without any fishing tackle. Not that anyone seemed to be showing much interest in me or the van. When the noisy group eventually thinned and spread out along the bank things quietened down and I couldn't resist the growls of my stomach any longer. I looked in the driver's mirror and saw the bags under my eyes and stubble coating my jaw. I was doing my best to straighten up when I spotted a grey toilet block almost hidden in the undergrowth and decided to pay a call. The place stank but at least it had running water to splash over my face and swill around my stale mouth. I felt marginally better, even if I didn't look it.

The couple in the hotdog trailer looked wary, probably guessing I'd been here all night. They served me politely enough but didn't seem overly bothered to make small talk. That suited me fine, and I took an egg and bacon roll, and polystyrene cup of strong black coffee back to the van. The early sun was giving way to cold, grey clouds and I wondered, not for the first time in my life, what on earth the attraction was in fishing. I just didn't get it – paying money to sit out in the cold and maybe catch nothing all day when, if you wanted fish, it could be bought cheaply enough in the market.

As I ate I also wondered what the hell it was in the back of my van that was so precious if it wasn't guns or drugs as Winsome assured me. By the time I'd finished the coffee my mind was made up and I unlocked the doors. The six boxes were all sealed with brown parcel tape and had no labels or markings. On one of the boxes the tape had curled up a little so I carefully prised it open until I could lift the cardboard flap inside and see the contents. There were more cartons inside packed tightly together. Judging by their size, I estimated there were probably about twenty in each box. I tore the corner of the outer box until I could remove one of the cartons, knowing I had more parcel tape in the glove compartment to repair it when I'd finished.

To my astonishment, the box had a picture of a toy plastic lorry with a plastic shipping container on the back. Maybe they were deliberately innocent looking to hide more sinister contents. Taking care not to damage the carton, I opened the lid and sure enough, inside was a plastic toy lorry looking exactly like the illustration on the outside. Its bright yellow plastic container was removable and was moulded to look like the kind of containers in use the world over to ship goods. The toy lorry was held in position by black plastic ties which I didn't dare to break. I shook it and it sounded empty. I placed the carton back inside the box and resealed it with the parcel tape. I stood back to examine my handiwork, satisfied that on a cursory inspection no one would ever suspect the box had been tampered with.

I picked up each of the other boxes in turn. They all felt a similar weight and I felt sure the other boxes held the same toys. What I couldn't figure was why that entire cloak and dagger melodrama with guns and a midnight rendezvous were necessary to protect a consignment of toys? Whoever the men they'd met last night were, they definitely didn't look like Santa's little helpers to me! It was a puzzle.

I climbed back into the cab and checked the mobile phone; still no messages or indications of a missed call. I scrolled through the contacts and wondered whether or not I should instigate a call to Winsome or Leon but I'd been told to lay low and wait for a call, so decided to stay put and give it a little bit longer. A few more fishermen arrived and all of them seemed keen to have coffee and a roll before starting to fish. I guessed they'd be back for more sustenance mid-morning, and probably again for lunch and concluded that the vendors were probably making a tidy sum.

My patience was running out when suddenly the mobile rang making me jump.

"Hi Marty, where are yer, mate?"

I felt relieved to hear Winsome's voice.

"I'm in a car park up by the reservoir."

"You been there all night?" Winsome sounded incredulous.

"You told me to lay low, and that's what I did. What the hell went wrong last night? Are you and Mike OK?

What am I supposed to do now with this stuff in the van? Where the hell are you anyway? How did you get away?"

"Whoa, easy tiger! Don't panic now, you did really well to get away last night."

"I've had a shitty night worrying myself sick. What the fuck's going on?"

"All in good time, Marty, all in good time. Mike and me are just fine, nothing to worry about. Stay right where you are. We're on our way and should be with you in about five minutes. And then I promise we'll tell you everything. OK?"

"OK."

As I ended the call I thought I heard Mike in the background laughing. What they had to laugh about God only knew.

It was ten minutes before Mike's 4x4 rolled smoothly into the car park and pulled alongside me.

"Jesus! Yer look rough!" were Winsome's opening words of greeting.

"I feel it," I said. "So what happened last night?"

"All in good time," Winsome said, glancing at the hot dog van, "but let's get some coffee first, shall we? I'll buy 'em, you go and sit with Mike."

Mike grinned at me as he climbed into the 4x4. "Alright mate?" he said.

"I am now," I said. "Did those guys hurt you last night?"

Mike grinned at me again, "Nah," he said, shrugging his big shoulders.

Winsome returned with the coffee and handed mine to me through the window.

Just as I took a sip, another van sped into the car park and pulled up right alongside us. It was the same two men from last night.

I spluttered coffee. "Fucking Hell," I cried, "they must've followed you here!" In my excitement I spilled more coffee into my lap and cursed some more.

The two men had already jumped out of their vehicle and suddenly they all burst out laughing. Winsome was doubled up with the pain of laughing and the others all had tears in their eyes.

The slow dawning of realisation came to me that I'd been had. "You fucking bastards!" I said, wanting to laugh along with them but feeling much too angry to join in. "What the fuck?"

"The look on yer face!" Winsome said, still clutching his side and trying to control his spasms of laughter. "And now it looks like yer've pissed yerself too!" he cried, pointing at my crotch.

Actually, the hot coffee had scalded me, but I was damned if I was going to give them a cause for even more mirth, so I just gritted his teeth and tried to smile.

"You bastards," I muttered, "you really had me fooled!"

I looked from Mike to Winsome and then at the other two guys and said again, "You're all bastards – the lot of you!"

Winsome made the introductions, "Marty, this is Colin and Ian. Guys, meet Marty the banker – and no, before one of yer says it, that ain't rhyming slang for wanker."

I grimaced, knowing that this was now the image that would nevertheless stick in Colin and Ian's minds. They shook hands warmly enough and both made strong eye contact with me and, despite my reservations, I found myself liking them.

"Colin and Ian both work for Leon too," Winsome explained, "sorry we had to put you through that, Marty me old mate, but it's like a kind of initiation ceremony that we all have to go through when we start working for Leon. Yer didn't think we'd take yer out on a proper job without testing yer mettle first did yer?"

I tried to hide my irritation. "So did I pass this initiation test?"

"With flying colours, Marty, yer did exactly what yer was told and kept yer cool. He was brilliant, wasn't he guys?"

They all agreed and slapped me a bit too heartily on the back and I started to feel my anger slipping away.

Winsome checked his watch and said, "Nearly opening time, let's go celebrate down the pub. Whadda ya think guys?"

Mike, Colin and Ian all nodded.

I would've preferred to go back to the flat and have a shave and a bath but felt it'd be churlish to refuse. "Why not?" I said. "I figure you all owe me one for pulling a stunt like that!"

They went back to their respective vehicles but before they got in Winsome grabbed me by the arm and said, "Just remembered one more thing we've gotta do!" he looked surreptitiously over his shoulder at the hotdog van and, satisfied that no one was watching he went over to my van and removed a set of magnetic false number plates.

I gaped at them open mouthed, unable to believe I hadn't spotted the switch when I'd been over for a coffee earlier.

"Just a precaution," Winsome explained. "When we're out and about we don't want traffic cameras flagging up our real numbers in case we're caught speeding, or jumping lights. That'd never do would it Marty?"

"Of course not," I said, trying to put a smile on my face. Inside I was seething. What the hell were they thinking of?

We left the car park in a convoy under the cold gaze of the hot dog vendor.

As I followed them, I pondered on what might've happened had that police car stopped me. Surely the first question they always ask is: "Can you tell me the registration number of the vehicle you're driving?" I would have given them my real number and then had to explain the false plates. Idiots! I felt my anger with them rising once again as I followed them back to the Old Dragon Inn where the adventure had all begun some twelve hours earlier.

I attracted a few curious stares from the locals but as soon as they saw who I was with people relaxed and went back to their own hushed conversations, or their games of dominoes and darts. It was a 'locals' bar where all strangers were viewed with suspicion. An almost impossible pub for anyone unknown, such as a police undercover officer, to eavesdrop on conversations.

None of my four new companions would allow me to buy a round but each of them in turn insisted on buying me a pint of beer. I wasn't particularly used to drinking before lunchtime and the four pints made me tipsy.

Winsome said, "We can't let you drive home in that state Marty. Give us yer keys and I'll drive yer home."

I reckoned that Winsome had had every bit as much to drink as me but I didn't feel like arguing so handed over the keys. Winsome drove perfectly with Mike following them in the 4x4.

"We'll drop yer at yer flat first Marty, yer look all in, then we'll take the van and unload the boxes back into the lock-up garage and bring the van back, leave it outside, and post yer keys through the letter box. OK mate?"

Winsome nearly always finished his instructions with a question as if checking that the message had been received and understood. I wasn't sure if this stemmed from thoroughness or insecurity, or both maybe.

When I finally closed my front door I went straight to the bedroom and flopped on the bed fully clothed and woke in exactly the same position several hours later.

It was the mobile phone ringing, the one Winsome had given me, which woke me. I swore I'd have to do something about the awful ringtone.

It was Leon. "Hi Martin, I heard the lads put you through their little initiation and you came through it well. Congratulations!"

"Thank you but was it really necessary?" I asked, still

irritated and with a headache now too.

I heard Leon sigh down the phone line before answering. "Martin, I've known you long enough and consider myself a good enough judge of character to trust you without putting you through any such tests of character. But for the lads, it was important to them to prove that you could be trusted in a crisis because what you do or how you act could have a big impact on their lives and possibly their freedom. Do you understand that?"

I thought about it, "Yes, I see that but I don't see what their silly little stunt proved."

"Think about it Martin, at the time it was not a joke for you, it was real. You could have panicked in the face of adversity, or become paralysed with fear, but you did neither. You might've driven straight to a police station and told them all, but you didn't. You might have taken it upon yourself to abscond with the goods in the back of your van which you clearly believed to be of high value, but you didn't. You could have driven straight back to your flat where, had the police been involved, they could easily have picked you and the goods up, but you didn't. You followed your instructions to the letter and in so doing proved yourself reliable and trustworthy to the guys. So I say again, congratulations, you did very well and have made friends who, now they know they can count on you, will reciprocate by never letting you down in a crisis. Tonight, Martin, you earned your spurs!"

I felt placated by Leon's words and touched by his faith in me. "Thank you," I said. "I hadn't seen it that way."

"You're welcome. Now, get a good night's sleep tonight because tomorrow night you'll be doing something similar but this time I promise you it will be for real and there'll be a large bonus for you by the end of the shift!"

With that Leon ended the call leaving me worrying yet again just what the hell I was getting into.

Then my personal mobile rang, and the name that came up on the caller display made the hangover feel worse.

"Hello Katrina," I said.

"I need money for a new washing machine; ours is broken beyond repair," she said, in her usual forthright way.

"Doesn't Tim have a machine you could use?"

"Don't be ridiculous Martin. I can hardly be seen carrying my laundry down the street. What would the neighbours think!"

I was tempted to say they'd think nothing of it compared to the brick Miriam hurled through the window but I just couldn't be bothered. Instead I said, "What's wrong with the local launderette?"

"For goodness sake, you just splashed out three hundred quid spending money for Ella's holiday to ingratiate yourself with her and now you begrudge me the same for a new washing machine."

"It's because I gave Ella that money that I can't dole out another lump sum so easily."

I hadn't told her about my working for Leon and was happy to let her believe I was still struggling with my new business, besides I hadn't actually received any pay yet from Leon. Then I remembered the promise of a bonus for tomorrow night.

"Look, Katrina, give me a couple of days and I'll see what I can come up with. Can you manage until then?"

"Do I have any choice?" she said and hung up.

CHAPTER SIXTEEN

The following evening came all too quickly and once again fear and adrenalin tied my stomach in knots. Earlier I'd been to the municipal tip and dumped the remaining junk from the back of the van so at least this time it would be empty.

I was told to meet Mike and Ian at the same lock-up garage as before and only hoped I could remember the way without Winsome sitting beside me giving directions. I took one wrong turn on the estate but soon retraced my path and found the place. Winsome was also waiting at the garage saying he'd help us load the van but wouldn't be coming to the meet.

This time there were about twenty boxes almost identical to those we'd taken on Saturday.

"What's in these?" I whispered to Winsome when the other two were out of earshot.

Winsome looked up at me, cocked his head to one side. "You mean you still don't know?"

I suspected this may be another test. "How would I know?" I said. "You told me it was better not to know. Don't you remember?"

I held Winsome's gaze until he smiled at me and I felt

like I'd just passed another test. "That's true," Winsome replied, "it's generally better not to know but I'll tell you if you want me to."

"Go on then." I had to satisfy my curiosity about why several boxes of toy lorries could possibly be so valuable and require night-time exchanges in deserted places.

"Toy trucks," Winsome pronounced.

I pretended to be upset. "Now you're just taking the piss!" I said.

Winsome grinned at me again plainly enjoying his position of knowledge. "Not just any old toy trucks though," he said, tapping the side of his nose, "these have special little containers with a built in secret compartment for smuggling. They get exported to places like Pakistan and Afghanistan, where they get filled and reimported into this country."

"I thought you said Leon doesn't deal in drugs?"

"Who said anything about drugs? They could be stuffing them with diamonds for all we know or care! Leon just supplies the toy trucks, no questions asked."

I hoped the disapproval didn't show on my face. I remembered my conversation with Leon about lines being crossed and wondered, not for the first time, where exactly Leon did draw the line.

Once again, we went through a similar process as before, loading the boxes onto the van and I watched Mike and Ian push pistols into the back of their waistbands. In a strange way the rehearsal, as I now looked upon my initiation, had served me well as a training exercise because I was altogether less fazed even though it was for real this time.

I even placed the false plates on the van myself and memorised the number just in case I needed to recite it if stopped. The rendezvous point was a very similar site but on a different industrial estate and we drove around the block a couple of times looking for any possible surveillance vehicles before turning into the area and committing to anything. A few minutes later another van similar to mine did much the same thing. I couldn't help wondering if the occupants of that van were similarly armed and if it too bore false plates.

This time there was no animosity between the parties, money was handed over and counted, and then the other van backed up to mine so that they were end to end and the boxes were quickly transferred. I remained in the van with the engine running ready to bolt if needed. The whole episode passed without incident and lasted no more than ten minutes from start to finish.

I still felt a certain amount of relief that it was over and sensed an easing of tension in Mike and Ian too. We were back at the lock-up by ten past one in the morning so it wasn't going to be too late a night either. Before I stepped out of the van, Mike opened the briefcase and handed Ian and I a wad of notes each.

"Bonus time!" he said.

Ian just nodded and slipped the envelope into his inside pocket. I did the same but I reckoned there was at least a few hundred pounds in mine: not bad for an hour's work!

I put the false plates back and drove home, glad not to have to be spending another long night in a deserted lay-by.

*

Next morning, I decided to surprise Katrina around coffee time and give her the washing machine money. My spirits were high until I saw Tim's car parked on my drive. I contemplated turning the van around when I saw Katrina looking out of the window at me. When she opened the door she didn't seem eager to invite me inside.

"This is a surprise," she said. "What brings you here?"

"I've brought you some money for the washing machine."

"Oh, thanks," she opened the door a bit wider, "you'd better come in then I suppose."

I wasn't bowled over by her enthusiasm.

"Tim's here," I observed, trying to sound neutral.

With that, he appeared from behind the kitchen door with a mug of coffee in his hand.

"Hello, Martin, can we get you a cup of coffee?"

"Sure," I said, "and why don't I make myself at home too?"

Tim looked nonplussed.

"You're welcome to stay, Martin, but only if you can be civil to Tim," Katrina cut in quickly.

"In that case, I'll pass on the coffee and go on being uncivil if that's OK with you."

Tim turned around and went back outside without another word.

"Was that really necessary?" Katrina asked.

"Yes," I said. "Has his car been on our drive all night? What will the neighbours think about that?"

For the first time in as far back as I could remember, Katrina seemed at a loss for words and just shrugged her shoulders.

"Here," I said, thrusting five fifty pound notes into her hands, "for a new washing machine."

"Thanks, Martin," she said, "and... sorry Tim was here. If you ring next time you come around he'll make himself scarce, I promise."

I looked at her and couldn't help wondering how many more times I'd be 'coming around'. I nodded briefly and then climbed back into the cab without another glance her way but when I checked the wing mirrors I saw her standing in the doorway, watching me go with a strange, almost wistful look on her face.

*

I hated having nothing to do and no one to talk to. Having turned down a coffee with Katrina and Tim, I decided to go to Beth's Café for a late breakfast. The place was busy and Beth only really had time to say a quick hello and ask me if I could deliver a buffet for her the next day. After pushing the last of my fried bread around the plate and finishing the coffee, I went for a walk in the park. This job still felt alien to me. I'd entered such a different world from the bank and found having so little to do tiresome. It gave me too much time to dwell upon the odd jobs I'd been given and once again doubts plagued me about what I was getting into with Leon. I didn't much care for this life filled with fast and slow times, peaks and troughs, highs and lows.

CHAPTER SEVENTEEN

Back at the flat I flicked the TV on more for company than for any desire to see another antiques or house renovation programme. I switched to a 24-hour news channel and then went into the kitchen to fill the kettle for a cup of tea. I wasn't really listening so when I came back I was surprised to see a photo of Ian, one of the guys from last night's job. He was only on the screen for a few seconds before they cut to another familiar face. Detective Inspector Bruno Cannard was standing outside the Old Dragon Inn where blue and white police tape fluttered in the breeze. He was appealing for anyone who witnessed 'this appalling crime' to come forward and a telephone number flashed across the bottom of the screen as he spoke. Then the news anchor woman moved on to the next story about some river that had been polluted.

I reached for the remote control to rewind the story and then threw it back onto the armchair in frustration when I realised I no longer had my fancy HD digital box that could pause and rewind live TV. I turned on my laptop to check the news on the Internet instead.

The story had made the national news but the most detail was on the local news pages:

Local Business Man Shot Dead

Local businessman, Ian Walters, 35, was found shot dead this morning in the Old Dragon Inn which he owned in the Canton area of Cardiff. His body was found by staff arriving to open the pub for the lunchtime trade and it is not clear yet how long the body had been lying there. Police are treating the death as suspicious and Detective Inspector Bruno Cannard is appealing for anyone who may have seen or heard anything, or spoken to the deceased in the last 48 hours, to come forward. Walters leaves a wife and two small children.

I felt numb with shock. Although we'd only just met, I recalled his wicked smile and the twinkle in his eyes when he'd shown me photographs of his young toddler son and baby daughter while we sat in the Old Dragon. I'd had no idea at the time that Ian was the owner of the place.

I needed to talk to someone and looked at the office mobile phone willing it to ring. It didn't, of course, so I called Winsome.

He answered so quickly I didn't even hear the ringing tone and just said, "What's up, Marty?"

"I was hoping you could tell me that. I just heard the news about Ian."

"Yeah, rum business that."

"So what happened?"

"Not on the phone," Winsome said. "I was gonna call yer anyway, we've got another special delivery for yer this afternoon. Do you know that park near the church at the bottom of Waterloo Road?"

"Yes."

"Be there in fifteen minutes."

I started to reply but I was already talking to a dead line.

Eleven minutes later I parked near the entrance to the park opposite the hall where Ella had gone to Brownies so many years ago, but in some ways like yesterday. There was no sign of Winsome so I sat and waited in the van. A few minutes later there was a tap on the passenger door and Winsome's craggy features appeared at the window. He climbed into the cab next to me and put a small parcel into the glove compartment.

I was eager to talk but Winsome put a finger over his lips and said, "Not here, let's take a walk in the park."

"Yer may think all this cloak and dagger stuff is a bit over the bleedin' top," Winsome began, "but we 'ave to be careful what we say and where we say it – we know the police suspect Leon's some kinda gangster, even if nothing could be further from the truth."

I let that one go.

"Fact is," Winsome continued, "we don't think Ian was hit just for the money from last night's deal, which is missing by the way, but also because someone's trying to muscle onto our turf and we've a pretty good idea who."

"We do?"

"Yeah, we think Ian may've been shot by one of Harry Rodgers' boys."

"With the gun I delivered?" I closed his eyes and swallowed back the bile rising in my throat.

"Yeah."

"Oh God, my fingerprints were all over that package!"

Winsome raised an eyebrow, "So what, unless they're on the shooter itself, that don't prove shit."

"But how can you know it was that gun? Surely that'd take forensic experts days to establish!"

"We don't need forensics, we've got the gun, it was left at the scene and the barmaid who found Ian 'ad the good sense to pick it up an' hide it before the cops arrived."

I replayed in my mind the serious consequences of tampering with evidence at a murder scene. What Winsome said next made my blood cold.

"In fact, it's in the glovebox of yer van right now."

"Bloody hell!" I spun around ready to run back to the van and felt a restraining hand on my arm.

"Just calm down, Marty and don't panic!"

"That's easy for you to say! What the fuck am I supposed to do with it?"

"Well, Marty, it's no use now it's contaminated. No one wants to hire a shooter that's been used in a murder – coz if yer caught with it yer may be implicated. So all yer gotta do is take a nice long drive into the countryside an' find a deserted stretch of river. Just pull over like you've stopped for a pee, make sure no one's about, and then toss the bloody thing into the middle of the river. What could be simpler? Yer don't even 'ave to get a signature this time," he added, winking at me.

I didn't like it. Surely this was making me an accessory-after-the-fact, or something. I was positive if I were caught I'd go to prison, or worse, like Winsome said, they may think I was the murderer!

"I don't know about this," I said.

"What?" Winsome said, failing to hide his irritability.

"I don't understand why we'd want to destroy evidence that might help convict Ian's killer."

"One," Winsome began counting off on his fingers, "whoever did this is a pro so they wouldn't leave no prints on the shooter. Two, 'ow do we explain, at this late stage, 'ow it came into our possession. Three, we have our own way of dishin' out justice to killers an' it's a bloody sight quicker and more efficient than any court of law – *and* it saves taxpayers' money!"

I could tell any further objections would be futile.

"Any particular river in mind?" I asked.

"That's more like it," Winsome said, revealing his crooked teeth. "I don't wanna know where – then I can't tell no one. It'll be yer own little secret, Marty. Just make sure you toss it somewhere where it'll never be found in our lifetime, OK?"

*

I drove miles further than I probably needed to. I had no idea where I was going and no memory of the roads I took or the villages I passed through. My mind drove on autopilot while my thoughts took me round in circles. Soon I found myself meandering down lanes somewhere in the Welsh Marches criss-crossing over the river Usk. Eventually, I came to a stretch of road that ran parallel with the river. The traffic was sparse and the banks of the river were lined with trees. I pulled into a lay-by hidden by a high hedgerow from the road. There were a few picnic tables and some barbecue stands dotted here and there. This would be a popular spot on the weekends but today, thank goodness, there wasn't another car in sight.

I took the package from the glove compartment and it weighed heavy in my hands. A path led away from the picnic spot toward the bank of the river. I followed it until I passed by what looked like a deep pool in the river. Standing still, I cocked my head to one side to listen. All I could hear was the river tumbling over rocks and a few birds or small rodents rustling in the shrubs. I checked for dog-walkers, fishermen, canoeists or anyone else that might disturb me. A lone heron stood a little further down the bank and I took that as a good sign that no one was around the corner. Satisfied I was alone I readied myself to toss the gun into the centre of the pool. But then I hesitated as Winsome's comment about guns being useful 'insurance' made me think. Thoughtfully, I retraced my steps back to the van, gun still in hand.

I didn't have a shovel with me but fortunately there'd been some recent rain and the ground was soft. A flat piece of wood from a broken pallet may be enough to dig a sufficient size hole. I found an oily old rag in the toolbox which I hoped might prevent the gun from rusting. I also had some empty supermarket carrier bags in the glove compartment. I wrapped the gun carefully before heading back along the path. I chose a spot, high enough to avoid the river in flood and far enough into the undergrowth so as not to attract any would-be treasure hunter with a metal detector, and started digging. After the gun was safely buried I took a good hard look around the place committing the various landmarks to memory so I would always be able to find it again.

I could hardly believe what I'd just done. I was a little comforted that if I ever needed something on Leon I had some 'insurance' of my own. Yet a part of me, the law abiding part, was horrified that I'd just hidden a murder weapon. All I wanted now was to get away from the place and return to the safety of my flat.

My van was still the only vehicle in the lay-by and it was hidden from the road so with luck no one will have seen it. When I pulled out of the lay-by there were no other vehicles on the road in either direction so no witnesses to say they saw me in the vicinity. I thanked my lucky stars and pointed the van towards home.

It was dark by the time I got to the flat and I was exhausted. On my way home, on impulse, I'd stopped at an off-licence and bought a bottle of five-star brandy. I'd been avoiding booze since the separation, afraid to start drinking alone but tonight I needed it more than ever and poured a generous measure.

The golden liquid spread warmth through my body. I finished the first glass in minutes and poured another but before taking a sip, I screwed the top back on tightly and placed the bottle out of sight in a cupboard in the kitchen. I managed to make the second glass last half an hour and ate a packet of cashew nuts while watching some late night extreme sports programme about surfers in shark-infested waters. I felt a kind of affinity with them as metaphorically, I too was swimming with sharks.

I sank into bed but tossed and turned for ages before drifting asleep. When I did, I dreamt Leon was watching me bury the gun from the bushes when, for some reason his mobile rang and rang but he didn't answer it. Then I realised it was mine. My eyes refused to focus on the caller display and "Huh," was about as close to hello as I could manage.

"Dad, is that you, did I wake you?" her voice was

slurred.

I was wide awake now hoping Ella wasn't in some kind of trouble.

"It's OK," I lied. "I'd only just got into bed."

The hands of my alarm clock glowed.

"It's nearly two o'clock, Ella, where are you? Is everything alright?"

"Sorry."

She let out a loud, unlady-like burp before continuing, "I didn't realise it was so late. We're having a party."

"You having a good time?"

"Yes, great thanks. We're at Leon Cooper's vineyard – you never told me your new boss owned a vineyard!"

I felt the hairs at the nape of my neck rise and I shivered. I had no idea Leon owned a vineyard and said so.

"He says he inherited it from his French mother," Ella continued.

"He says what? You mean he's there with you now?"

"Of course, silly! Hold on, he wants a word."

The next voice I heard was Leon's.

"Martin, you didn't tell me your daughter was such a beautiful young woman," he purred down the line making me feel sick.

Had he been drinking too?

"You never told me you owned a vineyard," I retorted.

Although I couldn't see him, I sensed him giving one of his Gallic shrugs.

"Don't worry Martin, Ella is a little tipsy but I have told her and her friends they can stay the night in my chateau so they'll all be perfectly safe."

"When did you go to France?" I asked trying to think when I last saw him.

"It was an impulse, I flew out yesterday. Wait a minute, Ella wants to talk to you."

"Hi Dad, it's me again. I just wanted to tell you how sorry I am that you and Mum are splitting up. It really, really makes me soooo sad..." her voice tailed off.

"It is sad, honey," I said, "but it's for the best." Did I really believe that, I wondered. "But I don't like to think of it spoiling your holiday, my lovely."

"I love you, Dad."

"I love you too..."

And just like that she was gone. Maybe it was just the drink making her maudlin. Now I was more worried about her than ever; I didn't like it one bit that she had 'encountered' Leon. Was it coincidence? Or was there something more sinister going on? Needless to say, I couldn't get back to sleep.

CHAPTER EIGHTEEN

The next morning I had a delivery for Beth. She poured me a coffee and sat while I drank it.

"Are you OK? You look tired."

She leaned across the table and ran her fingers across the bags under my eyes. Her touch was cool on my skin.

"Trouble sleeping last night," I admitted. "Ella rang me from France. She and her friends stayed over at Leon's chateau last night. She was a little bit tipsy and upset about you know... me and..." It was no good, I had to stop as tears welled in my eyes. I bit my lower lip fighting back the urge to sob. One kind word now from Beth and the floodgates would open.

She seemed to sense this and to spare me further embarrassment she simply patted the back of my hand and said, "You look like you could use a good breakfast to me – I'll make you up a house special."

I mouthed a thank you to her and dabbed my eyes with a paper serviette.

I was grateful that she'd steered me to a quiet table in the corner of the cafe where I could sit relatively unobserved. I hadn't realised just how upset Ella's call had made me. Leon's involvement scared me. I felt I'd somehow let Ella down. Katrina's betrayal had cut into my very core and hurt me so much I wasn't sure I'd ever recover. Yet how could I just stop loving someone I'd shared the bulk of my adult life with – Katrina was such a big part of all my memories. It felt like a kind of bereavement. In my heart I'd been aware that Katrina and I weren't as close as we once were, but I always thought it was fixable. Catching her with another man had been such a shock and that it was someone I knew, and didn't really like very much, made it worse. Then I found out they'd been seeing each other behind my back for some time. It was the fact she could lie to me with such a straight face, that's what hurt the most. It was that, even more than sleeping with another man, that I felt most unforgivable.

Beth returned with a huge fried breakfast that I really didn't feel like eating.

"Get that down you and you'll forget all your problems, I guarantee it. Trust me, I've been through a divorce myself and, although it may not seem like it right now, you will come out the other side and be stronger for the experience."

That took me by surprise. "How long ago were you divorced?" I asked.

"About ten years ago, not long before I opened this cafe. I was married to the boss, so not only did I lose my husband, I lost my job too, just like you've done. I used the settlement money to set up this place."

"You've done well here," I said.

"It's true what they say, Martin, what doesn't kill you strengthens you."

"Thanks, Beth."

"You will pull through the divorce. In the meantime," she added enigmatically, "I just hope working for Leon Cooper doesn't get you killed!"

"I'll take care, I promise you."

"Just remember that when criminals fall out it's the foot-soldiers who are the first pawns to be sacrificed. Did you know that man who was shot?"

I nodded.

She laid a hand on my forearm and said, "Watch your back, is all I'm saying," and then she moved off to serve another customer.

*

After completing the deliveries I returned to the flat and had just finished making a cup of tea when the doorbell rang.

It was DI Bruno Cannard, "Hello Martin, mind if I have a quick word?"

"Sure." I stood frozen to the spot.

"Well, are you going to let me in then?"

I backed away, allowing the inspector to enter. He walked down the hall, looking around him, taking in all the details and I suddenly felt ashamed of how untidy it was.

Seeing the full cup of tea Cannard rubbed his hands together and said, "Ooh, is there any more of that in the pot?"

I poured a mug and handed it to him. He spooned in four sugars from the bowl and stirred.

"I'd have thought a man on your income could have afforded something better than this," Cannard observed.

"What, having just been made redundant and separating from my wife, you mean?"

Cannard gave a humourless smile, "Oh, believe me I know how costly divorce can be," he said. "I've had two of them and they both took me to the cleaners! All the same, you've fallen on your feet. I heard you've landed a nice little earner working for Leon Cooper."

Leon's warning to say nothing rang in my ears. "No comment; how I earn my money is my business," I said.

"As long as you earn it legitimately," Cannard replied, "otherwise it becomes my business too."

Cannard scanned the flat, there wasn't much for him to see.

"You got any hobbies, Martin?" he asked.

"I watch a bit of football."

"Ever play?"

"Sunday league when I was younger."

"What about fishing? You ever go in for anything like that, Martin?"

I wondered where this was heading, I was sure no one had spotted me near that river bank in Shropshire.

"Nope, never been interested. Why do you ask?"

"Can you remember what you were doing two weeks last Sunday morning?"

"I can't hardly remember what I did this morning," I said, wondering where this line of questioning was heading. "I certainly wasn't fishing."

"Only a couple of weeks ago someone thought they spotted a van abandoned in the reservoir car park. They reckoned it had been there all night and were about to call it in when to their surprise the driver, who incidentally matched your description, got out and bought a breakfast roll. Ring any bells with you, Martin?"

I gave what I hoped looked like a non-committal shrug.

"They're a right pair of busybody nosey parkers those two, mind you, there's all sorts goes on in these car parks late at night so I suppose they're just protecting their patch really."

"Even if it was me, have I broken any laws?"

"Hell no, at least not eating a breakfast roll, but the thing is he's got a little black book full of vehicle registration numbers that use his car park, like a bloody train-spotter if you ask me. Except he keeps pestering us with his suspicions. Now the funny thing is that the first number he took down from the front of the van was registered to a small building firm in Manchester, but when the van was driving out he noticed it had a different number on the back registered to you. So that's when he reported it. What do you make of that now, Martin, odd isn't it?"

"You've jogged my memory now," I said, thinking fast,

noticing Cannard's eyes narrowing, "it was me, I'd done a late delivery and was so tired I thought I'd pull off the road and snatch forty winks before driving home. You know, 'tiredness can kill' and all that. Next thing I knew it was morning and I was woken by a flock of geese and some early morning fisherman having breakfast."

"Oh yes, and what do you make of the different number plates on the front and back of your van?"

"Well he obviously made a mistake, Inspector, the van's parked right outside. You can come and check for yourself if you'd like to."

"It's OK, I already have done," Cannard said. "Funny though, all the years that guys been noting numbers and I've never known him get one wrong before. Still, he's not getting any younger I suppose. Maybe it's time he bought some spectacles!"

"Well, I'm glad we've solved that little mystery. Is there anything else I can do for you, Inspector?"

"No thanks, I think we're done here," Cannard drained his mug of tea.

He stood to leave but as he got to the door he turned and said, "That bloke who was shot, Ian Walters, did you know him?"

The question threw me and I decided it was probably safe to admit knowing him by sight. "Not well, but I may have seen him before when I've had the odd pint in the Old Dragon."

Cannard's piercing eyes met mine again and he said, "The Old Dragon Inn isn't the kind of place where you find many bankers going out for a drink."

"I'm not a banker any more. Remember? I'm a white van man."

"Hmmm... Take good care of yourself, Martin. So long for now." With that he turned and left.

That's two people who'd warned me to take care of myself in one day, I thought. Then my mobile rang and

Patrick's name flashed on the screen.

"Patrick! Hi!"

"Er, hi Martin, I wondered if you fancied a pint tonight, catch up on some news?"

It was great to hear a friendly voice. "I'd love to," I said, without hesitation.

"I'll drop by and pick you up about eight o'clock then and we'll go to the Rose and Crown, if you like."

Now that is more of a bankers' kind of pub I thought happily. "Great, see you later."

∗

Happily tucking into pie and chips from the bar menu, Patrick and I munched away in quiet contentment. Before the meal Patrick brought me up to date with the latest office gossip, but I couldn't help feeling there was something he was not telling me.

A barmaid cleared away our plates and I went to buy our next round.

When I returned Patrick started to say something in his stuttering way but then changed his mind.

"Come on, spit it out, you've been trying to tell me something all night. What is it?"

"D-D-Darren Pierce had a v-visit this morning from two plain clothes policemen."

I wondered what was coming next.

"T-The thing is when Sharon took them in a tray of coffee and biscuits she came out saying Pierce had turned the screen around to show something to the officers and she saw your name on the screen. It's a blatant abuse of the Data Protection Act and typical of Pierce to ride roughshod over the rules when it suits him," Patrick said, disapprovingly. "I just thought you should know about it, that's all."

He sat back looking at me for a reaction.

I tried to keep my face impassive, as I realised how Cannard had made some snide reference to me falling on my feet working for Leon Cooper. He must have seen some of the pay cheques from Leon in my account, so he already knew the answer, the cunning bastard.

"Er... look Martin, is there something you're up to that I should know about? I mean are you in cahoots with Leon Cooper?"

That told me that Patrick had also subsequently looked at my account but I couldn't blame him; I'd have done exactly the same.

I decided to come clean with him.

"I'm working for Coopers Logistics," I said. "Leon Cooper made me an offer that was too good to refuse."

Patrick almost choked in his beer. "You're making him sound like the Godfather!" he spluttered.

I silently admonished myself for the poor choice of words. "I didn't mean it like that," I said. "It's just that, well let's just say he improved on the salary the bank were paying me."

"So you picked up all that redundancy money and walked straight into a better paid job — wow! Well done you, I hope you know who to come to if you want any financial advice," he joked.

"You always said I was a lucky so and so!"

"So what's he got you doing for him? I'm guessing he can't be paying you that sort of money just to drive a van."

"Well, I do still drive the van a bit. He's even allowed me to keep my existing customers like Beth's Café, but obviously, there's a lot more to my role in his organisation than that. It's still early days yet but I think he's using my skills in a sort of generalist trouble-shooting role."

OK so I was bigging myself up to my old friend and felt mildly guilty about it.

Patrick's next question was the tricky one. "So what has he got you doing and why are the police so interested in your account all of a sudden?"

"I don't really know," I said, truthfully.

"He's not getting you caught up in anything illegal, is he Martin?"

"Hell no! Nothing like that!"

As long as you don't count delivering guns, doing shady midnight deals selling corrupted toys to smugglers, and disposing of murder weapons, then I'm straight as a die, I thought. As I made the list in my head I could feel the skin on my face burning and knew I was blushing.

Patrick looked at me strangely, but said nothing.

I carried on, eager to fill the void. "The thing is, Patrick, Leon is very sensitive about his business information and one of the conditions of my employment is that I had to swear not to tell anyone anything about him or his business interests. Not even you, mate."

"Well ...," said Patrick, "it all sounds a bit cloak and dagger to me! But then you're a smart bloke, Martin, you know what you're doing and what you're getting into. All I ask is that you take good care of yourself and stay out of trouble."

That was the third time that day I'd been told to take good care of myself. It was starting to make me think long and hard about what I was doing for Leon Cooper.

The conversation was a bit stilted and so soon after that we left and he dropped me back at my flat.

I continued giving some thought to just how far I was prepared to go for Leon. As I was learning more, I was beginning to feel that Leon was willing to cross a lot further over the line of legality than he'd first implied when offering me the job. It worried me a great deal that Ian had been shot in what appeared to be some kind of gangster turf war that he was caught up in. I didn't like what I was getting sucked into. It didn't take much intelligence to work out that I knew too much already to easily extricate myself from the men I was now working with. I didn't want to end up as 'cannon fodder', or, as Beth had suggested, a sacrificial pawn in someone else's chess game! I felt a cold fear grip my stomach and had to rush for the toilet.

At half past ten the work mobile rang and Winsome

said, "Get in your van, drop by the garage and put the false plates on, then meet me outside the Old Dragon in fifteen minutes. It's urgent."

"But ..." I began to protest but the phone was dead.

CHAPTER NINETEEN

After collecting the false plates from the lock-up, I found Winsome pacing up and down outside the Old Dragon. The police had removed the crime scene tape and the place looked the same as ever, except that since Ian had been shot it remained closed.

When he climbed into the cab the first thing he said was, "Yer not gonna like this job, Marty, not one bit, but it's gotta be done tonight and you're the only one available. So no arguments, OK?"

I didn't like the sound of this. "What the hell do you want me to do now?" I asked.

"Yer'll see soon enough. Tell me yer not one of these squeamish buggers that passes out at the sight of blood."

"For fuck sake! Now you're really starting to worry me!"

Winsome looked me up and down and said, "You'll be OK, just don't panic."

I could feel that familiar twinge in my guts and knew I'd need a toilet before much longer.

"Where are we going?"

"Harry Rodger's place. Can you remember the way?"

"I remember," I said, my stomach giving another

warning spasm. "I'm going to need to stop for a toilet break shortly; there's an all-night petrol station up ahead."

"You can't bloody go there!" Winsome said. "They'll have security cameras. There's a loo in the kebab shop up the road, use that if you must."

"I must," I replied, through gritted teeth.

I ran inside and nodded to the man behind the counter on my way through to the toilet. When I came out and made straight for the exit I heard him shout, "This is not a bloody public convenience!"

"You alright now?" Winsome asked.

"Why are we going to see Rodgers?" I asked, remembering how obnoxious the man was last time we'd met. "Has this got anything to do with Ian's murder?"

"Yes," Winsome replied, "everything to do with it!"

"Oh shit!" I said, easing my foot off the accelerator, slowing the van down.

"It's OK, you won't be in any danger, now come on, just drive."

Nothing moved at this time of night in the village of Coed Manor. Rodgers' house was hidden from the road by a high hedge and a long drive. There were no lights and no cars to be seen.

From a plastic carrier bag Winsome pulled two paper suits of the kind I'd only ever seen crime scene investigators wear on TV shows. The anti-DNA suits were baggy to fit over normal clothing, with a hood and a mask.

"Put these on too," Winsome said, handing me a pair of blue plastic bags with drawstrings.

My hands shook as I fumbled on the over-shoes. I followed Winsome to the front door of the house on trembling, unsteady legs. The door was open, as if we were expected.

Winsome wouldn't allow any lights so we used flashlights to move from room to room

Then the beam from my torch played over the corpse of Harry Rodgers and I damn near passed out. I gasped and immediately felt Winsome's hand on my shoulder.

"It's OK Marty, just take some deep breaths and don't panic."

I started to protest but Winsome dug his fingernails into my shoulder and shook me hard. "Stay calm and take those breaths – c'mon, you'll be alright."

I looked down at the body of the man who'd refused to sign for the gun that was allegedly used to shoot Ian...

*

After we'd struggled to move the corpse into the back of the van, we scrubbed every visible drop of blood from the tiled kitchen floor until my knees ached. We left the dirty dishes in the sink, untouched.

Winsome sniffed the air and finally declared, "That'll 'ave to do."

I drove the van while my mind was elsewhere, blindly following Winsome's directions. I felt terrified of having some kind of traffic accident while carrying the body in the back. A cold trickle of sweat ran down my spine. This was ridiculous! What if we were stopped? As well as 'tampering with the evidence' I could now add 'disposing of the body' to my long list of crimes – I was going to prison for sure: Oh bloody hell!

"So what now?" I heard my voice trill.

"You just gotta drive him around in the back of yer van for a few weeks until we can gauge the heat generated by his disappearance."

"What?!" I spluttered. "I can't do that! In a couple of days his corpse will be stinking and disease ridden. I can't deal with that – I've got food to deliver tomorrow!"

Out of the corner of my eye, I caught Winsome chuckling.

"Had you going there, didn't I Marty?" he roared. "Just follow my directions and we'll be rid of 'im tonight and it'll be somewhere no one will find 'im; a favourite method of Leon's on such occasions."

"Jesus, you're nuts," I muttered, despising myself for

being so gullible.

Winsome's last words clearly suggested this wasn't the first time they'd disposed of bodies and suddenly a wave of fear spread over me as I thought again about the shit I was in. Pulling out now would place me in serious jeopardy – I was too aware of how Leon operated and that he'd think nothing of taking out a grunt like me, for I'm sure that's how he saw me.

We arrived at another small village about ten miles away from Coed Manor where the houses were similarly large and detached, and a good distance apart from their neighbours. We turned into the drive of one of them and at the end I could see another van which, to my surprise, bore the logo Cooper's Courtyards, another part of Leon's business empire. Two burly men greeted us and as we shook hands I noticed the dirt beneath their fingernails and felt their rough calluses.

Winsome saw me looking at the dark house and said, "The owners are away on a cruise, too posh to stick around and be bothered by landscapers remodelling their garden. Very convenient for us though, as it happens."

"It's all ready around the back," one of the men said. He had the look of a man who was used to heavy work and this was confirmed when, effortlessly, he dragged the body out of the van like a sack of potatoes. The other guy caught hold of the feet and they walked nonchalantly around the side of the property like they were carrying an old carpet.

The moon appeared from behind a cloud, bathing the garden in silver. The surreal landscape reminded me of pictures of World War One trenches. Deep drainage ditches ran across what I assumed was going to be a lawn. In an area close to a large conservatory, a mechanical digger stood like a silent sentinel adjacent to a deep pit with a pile of freshly dug earth next to it. They removed the plastic cover, "...to speed decomposition" Winsome explained, and tossed Rodger's body unceremoniously into the pit.

Winsome then surprised me by grabbing a handful of earth and casting it over the body saying, "Ashes to ashes, dust to dust, we commend this poor soul to your keeping Lord. May he rest in peace." He solemnly made the sign of a cross in the air. The four of us stood for a moment in silence on the edge, staring into the grave.

Then, back to his old self, Winsome said, "OK, lads, let's fill it in."

Although the house was a fair way from other properties, they didn't want to draw attention with the noise of the digger starting at night, so they began manually shovelling earth into the hole, giving spades to me and Winsome to share the load. One final hand remained uncovered with an accusing finger pointing at us. I sensed all of us, even Winsome, felt a little freaked by this. We hurried to shovel more earth over Rodgers' last accusing gesture.

"Tomorrow they've got a load of hardcore coming to cover this area and it'll all be tamped down to make a patio," Winsome explained, "and when Mr and Mrs Posh are sitting here eating their cucumber sandwiches with the crusts cut off and sipping their Earl Grey tea, they'll have no idea that a corpse is rotting away six feet beneath them." He gave a macabre laugh and when we all remained silent he sighed at us as if we had no sense of humour and said, "Ah well, our work here's done lads. Thanks for yer 'elp and 'ere's a little bonus for yer troubles." He handed them each a brown envelope.

Back in the van he gave another brown envelope to me and said, "C'mon let's go home. Well done mate!"

It was three o'clock in the morning when I crept into the flat, having first stashed the false plates back in the lock-up.

I dropped onto the bed exhausted but sleep wouldn't come. Apart from an occasional parking ticket and the odd speed camera, I'd never been involved in anything unlawful. I'd been a trusted bank official, regarded by some as a pillar of the community, until the financial crisis at least, and now, in the space of a few short weeks, I'd been involved in so many dubious things. I was worried sick and scared too – I'd just witnessed how ruthless Leon and his cohorts could be. I felt my jaw remembering the aches and pains from my first encounter with them in that deserted forestry lane.

I could see no way out. If I ran surely they'd track me down and kill me. And where would I run to? I'd heard of people who'd simply vanished like Lord Lucan and left their money untouched for years in dormant bank accounts. I'd often speculated just how people managed it but now I had first-hand knowledge of one way people 'disappeared'. How many of them were buried under suburban patios? A horrifying thought occurred to me then: we'd used Leon's firm to have some landscaping done in our own garden. Leon had insisted on doing it free of charge after a particular banking investment I'd recommended did well. It broke all the bank's rules accepting this 'gift in kind' without declaring it. Was that the start of the slippery slope on which I now found himself? And, oh God, what if there was a body under my own rockery?! If the police ever found out about the job I'd just been part of they'd surely dig up my own garden to check.

I began to sweat, even though the night was cool and my thoughts continued to spiral downwards.

CHAPTER TWENTY

The following morning Leon dropped by the flat in person.

"So you're back from France then," I said, stating the obvious.

"Your daughter and her friends are lovely girls," he said, "you must be very proud of her."

"I am," I said.

He looked at me sideways and said, "God, you look awful."

"Are you surprised?" I demanded. I still felt angry at being put through yesterday's ordeal, so angry that, temporarily, I forgot how unwise it was to piss off Leon. "You never said a bloody thing to me about disposing of bodies when we discussed this job! Sometimes your operations were only borderline legal you said. There's nothing bloody borderline about aiding and abetting murder by burying the bloody bodies under innocent people's patios!"

"You are understandably angry, Martin, please let me explain what all this is about and why I value your help and am placing so much trust in you," he held his hands up, palms open, like a supplicant begging forgiveness.

"My activities are borderline as I told you and, of course, I know that recently they have dipped well below what is acceptable behaviour into the downright criminal. It is not normally like this, Martin, I promise you. Despite what you may think of me, I am not a gangster but I do believe in business one has to be ruthless and that on occasion the ends justify the means. That man who was killed, Harry Rodgers, now he was a true gangster in every sense of the word and a cruel and evil man. His stock in trade was drugs, protection rackets and sex slavery, and I could tell you stories about him that would give you nightmares for years to come. Take your daughter, Ella," he sighed, "you'd be appalled by what this man does to young girls who are all someone's daughters."

I was fed up of hearing my daughter's name on Leon's lips but bit my tongue to remain silent.

Leon continued. "Not content with an already vast criminal empire, Rodgers was trying to muscle in on my business interests. That man who beat you up, Martin, he worked for me but he had been turned against me by Rodgers who was paying him with call girls and drugs to spy on my business affairs. He had to be dealt with."

"Is he under someone's patio too?" I asked.

Leon just smiled enigmatically and carried on. "When Rodgers found out his man had been rumbled he had Ian shot, probably did it himself because he enjoys killing. So you see my problem; tit-for-tat killings is never in anyone's business interests but that is how Rodgers operates so I had no choice but to stop this cancerous growth by cutting it out at its source. As you can appreciate, Martin, many have tried to get close enough to this man to do that and have failed. It took meticulous planning on my part and I could only use men I could absolutely trust. Winsome has been by my side ever since we were at school together and I know I could trust him with my life. When I heard you were the victim of the traitor in my midst and that you'd lost your job, I thought here is a man I know and trust with my investments and his reputation is impeccable. I knew that if you accepted the job I could trust and rely on you whereas, in my own organisation, there may have been others turned by Rodgers who would betray my trust.

"But I had no way of knowing that events would unfold this fast, and I am sorry we have had to toss you into the middle of all this without even having much chance to explain what is happening and why. I've been proved right in placing my faith in you Martin and you have not let me down once. I on the other hand feel I have let you down by putting you through all this torment."

Leon bowed his head.

I had to admit it was quite a speech but I felt I had to be honest with him.

"I am not at all happy about the criminal situations you have placed me in," I said. "We both know the risks involved and if I'd been caught I'd be looking at jail and my reputation in tatters. I promised you I'd never give away any of your secrets and I'll keep that promise. In any case, it would be impossible to admit any of this without implicating myself so you have that assurance in addition to my word. However, I do not wish to continue working for you anymore."

Leon looked pained.

"Ah, Martin, I appreciate how you feel and your honesty with me but please hear me out. With Rodgers out of the way, this business is over, things will settle down quickly now and a normal pattern will emerge again where the vast majority of my business deals are legitimate and above board and, if you would prefer, I will make sure you are not involved in any of the more dubious deliveries. Please reconsider your resignation as I truly need good people like you that I know I can trust and who have proved themselves to me."

I began to shake my head but Leon raised a hand to me. "No," he said, firmly, "I will not accept your resignation yet. You must sleep on it, at least. Give yourself some time off to think about it and let me have your decision in a couple of weeks time. I insist Martin."

And that was that. Leon made it clear that any more talk about leaving was over for now.

Abruptly, he changed the subject. "Are the police still bothering you?" He looked at me expectantly.

I decided to come clean as one could never tell from his questions how much he already knew. "I had another visit from DI Cannard."

"What did Inspector Duck want this time?"

"I don't know how because I certainly didn't tell him, but he's figured out I'm on the payroll of Coopers Logistics."

Leon clasped his hands in his lap and twiddled his thumbs while he thought for a moment then he said, "Ah well, I was hoping our association would remain secret for a bit longer but it was only a matter of time I suppose. He surely didn't come around here just to tell you he knew you were working for me, so what else did he want?"

"He, er..." I wondered how Leon might take this, "he asked me my whereabouts on the night Winsome and the boys set me up on that bogus meeting."

"And?"

"At first I said I couldn't remember, then he started sounding me out about hobbies, asking me if I ever went fishing. When I told him no, he said the hot dog guy at the reservoir car park where I spent the night was a suspicious so and so and always took numbers of vehicles in the car park, especially if they appeared to have been there all night. Apparently they get a lot of abandoned vehicles there."

I had Leon's full attention now. "So what did you tell him?" he asked.

"I pretended to remember then, and said I'd driven a long way that day making deliveries and although I was almost home I was so tired I pulled over for a short nap. The next thing I knew it was morning."

"Do you think he believed you?"

"I'm not sure," I answered truthfully, "it gets worse..."

"Go on," Leon was starting to look impatient now.

"He said the guy in the hot dog stall took the registration number from the front of the van when I was parked up and then he noticed when I drove out that there was a different registration number on the back of the van. Cannard said that the first number was for a van owned by some builder in Manchester while the second was mine, and could I please explain."

Leon's face went a shade of red. "What the fuck went wrong?"

"I had no idea that the plates on my van had been switched until Winsome and the lads swept into the car park laughing at me and he removed both the plates and put them in the back of his 4x4."

"Did the hot dog man see him?"

"No. I saw Winsome check he wasn't looking before he made the switch. I told him I wasn't happy that he'd switched them without even telling me."

"If this prick selling the hot dogs took your number he probably took theirs too," Leon observed, his face turning darker by the minute as he thought through the consequences.

"I would imagine he did. Cannard said he was like a train-spotter and had notebooks full of car registration numbers and was always ringing the police – I think they regard him as a well-meaning nutter."

"Those same false plates," Leon paused, "did you use them on the job last night?"

"Yes," I said, hanging my head as the enormity of what I'd done sank in.

I never saw the blow coming. As I lifted my head, Leon's open hand slapped my face so hard that the force of it knocked me clean off my feet. I remained on the floor where I fell, my cheek stinging and my eyes smarting.

"For fuck sake, Martin, I'm paying you to think on your

feet remember?" Leon's face was incandescent with rage. "And why wait until now to tell me this? Why didn't you call me straight away?"

"I..." I couldn't finish the sentence because Leon kicked me in the stomach.

"I can't fucking believe this," Leon continued. "You used false plates on a murder cover up that you already knew had been compromised and so if the van was spotted by anyone last night, you've provided the police with a link from the van to you to me. You fucking idiot!"

I braced myself for another kicking but it never came. When I dared to look, Leon appeared to be calming down and had sat on the chair.

"I'm sorry Leon, it won't happen again. I promise."

Leon ignored my apology. "And Winsome should've known better than to swap number plates in a public place in broad daylight – he and I need to have a talk right now!" he said, jumping up to leave.

"You stay out of sight for a while and if inspector bloody duck comes back you let me know immediately. Do you understand?"

"Yes, Leon."

"Good!"

Leon stomped out of the flat, slamming the door behind him.

I remained cowering on the floor for a few minutes until the pain in my stomach gradually subsided. I lifted my shirt and carefully felt my ribs, hoping that the kick had not done further damage to my recent fracture. It was red and sore but other than that I didn't think the damage was serious this time.

I'd never seen Leon so furious, and I hoped never to see that side of him again. The man was a psychopath! I decided to try and warn Winsome of the storm coming his way and reached for the mobile.

A few hours later Winsome limped into my flat. He had a bruise on his cheekbone. I didn't feel the need to ask how he came by it.

"Thanks for the warning, Marty, you're a star," he said.

"I've never seen him like that before; he was like a wild thing," I confided.

"He does have a bit of a temper, that's for sure but as long as he's red in the face and shouting at yer then all yer gonna get is a bit of a beating. It's when he goes real quiet he's at his most deadly, you can see an intensity in his eyes that would scare a ghost," Winsome said, thoughtfully rubbing the side of his knee.

He saw me watching him and said, "Aye, I've only been on the receiving end of that look once and that was when he did this to me."

"What did he do?" I couldn't help asking, even though I wasn't sure I really wanted to know.

"He chained me to the rear wall of his garage and then reversed his car into me. Broke both my legs; he crushed this one so bad I was lucky they didn't amputate. The other one wasn't so bad because the bumper was curved."

I felt physically sick at the thought of it. "But I don't understand, if he did that to you why did you stay with him? And why are you so loyal to him?"

"It was a long time ago now, we were late teens and had been best of mates through school. Then I let him down really badly and this is what he did to me – I deserved it – I think if we hadn't been such good friends before he would've killed me. He told me exactly what he was going to do to me and made me swear to tell his parents it was an accident. He made me agree this up front because, after he did it, I guess he knew I'd pass out with the pain.

"Just as well he did that because when I came around I was in hospital with a copper sitting beside the bed. We stuck to the story and in the end they didn't press charges. He's a clever bloke is Leon, see, he thinks of every angle before he acts. So sometimes when the rest of us mortals make mistakes, like I did changing over those plates in public, he gets frustrated."

I listened with a growing sense of horror as Winsome spoke of being 'lucky' that Leon didn't kill him, and that the only reason his other leg was saved was because the bumper was curved. Yet again it was my stomach that bore the brunt of all this pent up emotion and I had to rush to the toilet.

When I returned, Winsome had found my coffee, boiled the kettle and made us two mugs of coffee.

"What was it you did that you say deserved this treatment?" I felt it was a natural question but saw Winsome stiffen.

"Leon swore me to secrecy and I've never told a soul," he said. "In fact, I've told yer too much already so whatever yer do don't let on to him that we've had this conversation. It all 'appened a long time ago an' it's better left in the past. OK?"

"You can trust me not to say a thing, I promise you," I said.

"The worst sin in Leon's eyes is betrayal," Winsome leaned forward, his voice almost a whisper now, "I betrayed Leon – it was a kinda 'ménage a trois', without one of the parties knowing, you get my meaning?"

I nodded.

"We'll let's just say Leon forgave me but, the third party, well, she wasn't as lucky as me..."

There wasn't much I could say after that. Winsome told me the false number plates had already been destroyed and a new set of 'safe' plates were being crafted as we spoke. He also reassured me that he was pretty certain no one would have seen the van on the night they disposed of Rodgers and his companion, it being such a quiet village and all; so he didn't think there was much risk of anything coming of this little indiscretion, or of it ever tracking back to Leon.

After he left, I was certain of one thing; I had to extricate myself from this world. It wouldn't be easy and I had no idea how I was going to do it, but do it I must. I couldn't go on in a job like this where I was expected to operate outside of the law with such an unpredictable and dangerous boss who thought nothing of inflicting horrific violence on others. I felt afraid, but another emotion was also taking over and that was anger. How dare Leon just knock me to the ground and give me a good kicking? I wasn't going to let him get away with that and felt a new resolve and determination stirring inside me.

I got on the phone to Patrick from the bank because I couldn't do it alone.

CHAPTER TWENTY-ONE

I took a super-size pizza and some beers around to Patrick's flat and during the meal, I quietly studied my friend and realised how little I actually knew about him. In fact, I'd never heard Patrick talk about his personal life. He was always immaculately groomed, even his casual clothes had a certain cut and style about them unlike my baggy jeans and polo shirt.

"So how come you're living alone, Patrick?" I asked. "Don't you ever get lonely? I certainly do and I've only been doing it a few weeks."

Patrick didn't give much away in his answer. "I imagine it must be a big adjustment for you after being married for so long, but don't worry, you'll get used to it."

He warily made eye contact with me as if waiting for the next question.

"Have you always lived alone?" I persisted.

"Not always." He seemed to be choosing his words carefully. "I did have a partner for a while and we shared a flat for about four years but in the end it didn't work out. It was a long time ago and I've quite enjoyed living by myself since. I get lonely sometimes but not having to share a fridge or a bathroom does have its compensations."

"Did I know you when you were going through this split? I don't recall you ever mentioning it."

"It was about eight years ago. We'd only just started working together – besides, I always try to keep my personal and professional lives apart."

I waited, hoping he'd open up.

It worked. "Like you, my partner had fidelity problems," he said. "Another man – well a string of other men actually."

"I'm sorry Patrick, I didn't mean to pry," I said, struck by the hurt I saw still lingering in his eyes.

"It's OK, you may as well hear the rest now," he said. "You see, the trouble with my partner was he simply couldn't keep his dick in his trousers and I was worried that with his hedonistic and rather incautious approach both of us would end up contracting AIDS. We had a big row and parted, and the next time I saw him was in a hospice shortly before he died, pretty much as I predicted though on that occasion I took no pleasure from being right."

I studied his face as if for the first time.

"God Patrick, we were sat next to each other all day while you were going through this and I never even noticed." I felt mortified. "I feel so insensitive and ashamed! I'd have been there for you if you'd opened up, I hope you know that."

"I do know that, Martin, but in all truth there was nothing you, or anyone else, could have done. He was on a road to self-destruction and I wasn't prepared to travel any further along it with him. After we split, I had tests and fortunately I'm clear of HIV myself."

"All the same, Patrick, even if I couldn't change anything, you could have talked to me, you know."

"I had plenty of help and support from the gay community and it was quite nice to come to work and not talk, or even think, about it for a few hours each day."

"And you've not found anyone else since?"

Patrick shook his head. "I expect I will one day..."

"I had no idea..." I shook my head at my lack of awareness.

"That I was gay?"

I nodded dumbly.

"I came out to close friends and family years ago. To be honest it's easier to be out than not these days, it's almost trendy. But I chose to keep it from work because despite legislation and general awareness, as you know there are still a few bigots in the bank that would try and destroy my career just for the hell of it."

"Darren Pierce, to name but one!" I said.

"Precisely!"

"Thanks for confiding, and I promise you no one will ever hear about any of this from me."

I extended my hand and we shook hands rather formally and then spontaneously embraced. Afterwards, to lighten the air, I told him, "I think you're the first gay man I've ever hugged!"

"Don't worry," Patrick said, grinning, "you're really not my type! Now I'm sure when you called around here it wasn't to talk about my problems so what's bothering you?"

Somehow a real divide had been crossed between us. Patrick was a truly close friend now and not just a friendly work colleague. It made it much easier for me to say what I had to. I told Patrick everything that had happened since I was beaten up in the forest, holding nothing back from him. I saw surprise and concern cross his face but never a hint of judgement, or disapproval.

"So that's where I'm at," I said, after finishing all there was to tell. "I want to get away from this dangerous man but I simply don't know how to extricate myself and stay in one piece. The fact is I already know too much about him for him to ever leave me alone."

Patrick took a moment to consider this, then said, "It's

hard to see how you could have done anything differently once the chain of events started to unfold, without, as you rightly point out, placing yourself in danger. The only time you could probably have walked away was if you'd turned down the Faustian job offer – you know what they say, if it seems too good to be true..."

"I did at first, but then when vandals torched the van I felt I had no options," I said, hanging my head.

"Don't blame yourself; you were vulnerable and Leon knew that. And he's the sort of bloke who stops at nothing to get his own way. I wouldn't put it past the devious bastard to have been behind torching your van."

"God, Patrick, that never occurred to me before but you may well be right!"

We spent the rest of the evening talking up and over and around and through the situation but no immediate solution presented itself.

In the end, Patrick said, "Let me sleep on it. I'm sure between us we'll come up with a way through this. In the meantime, Martin, you have to continue in exactly the same way as you have up to now. It's important that Leon continues to think you're passive and trustworthy and reliable. He clearly thinks quite highly of you and the only way you're going to trap him is if you have his complete confidence. Do you think you can do that?"

"I'll try my best! What choice do I have?"

"None really," Patrick admitted.

*

Next morning, after the first unbroken night's sleep in ages, I decided to call into Beth's and have a full breakfast. She gave me her usual friendly greeting but it was evident she was rushed. Her business was thriving and I felt genuinely pleased for her. There was even a sign in the window advertising for staff. It was great to see someone prospering in such difficult economic times. How I would dearly love to come and work in such a cheerful place with Beth for company all day long. I was sure she was every bit as good with her staff as she was with her customers. Everybody loved her, and that included me.

It even crossed my mind for a fleeting moment to ask for the job myself, but how could I in my present predicament. The last thing I'd want to do is expose Beth and her business to the likes of Leon Cooper.

My mind drifted back to yesterday evening with Patrick. If anyone could find a way to help me out of this mess it was him. He was a bright bloke. In fact, as a colleague, I often had to suppress my own envy as he came up with bright idea after bright idea. It was easy to see why they chose to make me redundant and keep Patrick.

I became aware that Beth was standing waving a hand in front of my face.

"Ah, you're back then!" she said, with an amused look on her face.

"Sorry, Beth, I was miles away."

"I could see that – did you go anywhere nice?"

"I'll send you a postcard next time," I joked.

"Postcards are so last century, Martin, it's all blogs and social media these days. We've even got free Wi-Fi here now," she said, pointing to the black and white sign in the window.

"How long have you had that?"

"About six months, Martin. You really do spend most of your time in a different world, don't you!

"If you're serious about making something of this business of yours you need to get yourself a website. The vast majority of our new catering customers come through mine you know, that and spreading the word on Twitter and FaceBook!"

"I wouldn't know where to start with all that but it's clearly doing well for you!"

"I certainly am! And at the moment I've got not one, not two, but three deliveries I need you to do tomorrow, so I hope you're free."

"I've got an urgent meeting at number 10 Downing

Street with the Prime Minister to discuss the economy but I'll drop that for your deliveries as they're much more important to me."

I smiled and we momentarily locked eyes. Was it the heat in the cafe, or was she blushing? The spell broke. I had a second cup of coffee and after that couldn't really find an excuse to linger.

Apart from the odd bit of work Beth put my way, business was very quiet and there was no contact from Winsome which in a way I felt quite pleased about. I was playing solitaire on my phone when it rang in my hand making me jump.

"Hi Katrina," I said, recovering fast and wondering what she wanted now.

"Can you pick up Ella from Heathrow tomorrow? I know it's short notice but my car's playing up and the garage have said they can look at it tomorrow."

She never said 'Hi' or 'Hello' any more but I let it go. "I'd love to..."

"Oh great," she interrupted. "Thanks Martin, her plane gets in at 4.30 in the afternoon."

She hung up without saying goodbye.

I felt irritated as I'd been going to say 'I'd love to but I can't' because I'd just promised to do those jobs for Beth. Immediately, I rang her back and her phone went straight to voicemail which either meant she'd declined my call, or was on the line to someone else.

I left a terse message to call me back.

When she did so I deliberately didn't greet her and simply said, "Before you interrupted and then cut me off, I was going to say I can't do tomorrow, I already have a job to do and I can't let customers down now I'm running a business."

"I see, but you're happy to let Ella down?"

I resisted the urge to point out it was she who was letting her down.

"You can hire a car, I'll pay."

"But I can't do that. Tim's wangled some tickets to the opera and I'll never be back in time to get ready!"

"So there's nothing actually wrong with your car then!"

"Well..."

I could tell she didn't like be caught out in a lie. Maybe I was a bit more aware of her lies than I had been.
"The car does need a service and it sometimes won't start!" she said, indignantly. "Please Martin, can't you let your customer down just this once? For the sake of your only daughter?"

I hated that she was stooping to emotional blackmail now.

"No, I can't!" I said. "This is your mess, not mine, so you can sort it out!"

I hung up without a goodbye, just as she'd done earlier; two could play that game. I felt guilty about letting Ella down, even though it hadn't been my fault and promised myself I'd take her out for a meal soon and listen to all her holiday stories – at least those she felt able to share with her old man.

CHAPTER TWENTY-TWO

Harry Rodgers' disappearance made the front page of the local newspaper, which reported: 'Concerns are growing for the missing businessman who has not been seen for several days'. There was a photograph of his wife who'd just returned from a holiday in the Azores complaining that he hadn't turned up as arranged at the airport to meet her and no one knew where he was. The police didn't take her seriously at first, she claimed, but now they were appealing for anyone who knew of his whereabouts to call them.

I closed the paper. I knew exactly where he was but I wasn't about to call. I thought of Rodgers' wife waiting at the airport as Ella had been. At least she'd been picked up because she'd phoned to tell me she was home and that Mum and that 'awful man' had been there to meet her. Apparently, they were all dressed up ready to go straight to the opera and furious because the plane had been delayed an hour so they missed the whole of the first act. She said they'd barely spoken to each other or to her on the whole journey back from the airport. I'd roared with laughter and agreed to buy Ella a meal tomorrow night.

Then the mobile phone I didn't want to hear chirped

and Winsome's number appeared on the caller display.

"Marty me old mate, we've gotta another job on tomorrow night."

"I can't do it," I replied instantly, "I've promised my daughter I'd take her out for a meal tomorrow night."

That was met with a few seconds of silent disapproval at the other end of the line.

After what seemed like an age, Winsome said, "That's OK. We don't need you 'til about half past eleven and all good daughters should be tucked up in bed by then."

I had no real choice and knew if they'd wanted me earlier I'd have been expected to rearrange my night out.

"That's fine then," I gave a resigned sigh. "What are we doing?"

Winsome wouldn't be drawn. "Turn up tomorrow at the usual place and you'll find out," he said and terminated the call.

Damn it. I looked at the dead mobile in my hands. It'd spoil the evening with Ella because I'd spend the whole time worrying about what would be laying in wait for me later and having to keep half an eye on the time to make sure I wasn't late. Would it be disposing of bodies again? Or some crooked deal? My stomach was knotting again and I wondered if I should see a doctor about it. I considered postponing meeting Ella but I was really missing her and she had a busy social life and going out with her dad was pretty low in the pecking order so I left things stand.

I had a few more catering pack deliveries to do for Beth but was disappointed not to see her when I went to pick them up. The vacancy notice in the window had been taken down and I was told she was busy interviewing candidates.

Alone in my flat later I watched the early evening news. Harry Rodgers had a small mention at the end of the local news and there was an old photograph of him as a much younger slimmer man. He was scowling at the camera, looking as if he resented having his picture taken, and I wondered if he'd ever smiled in his life. The newsreader said there was speculation that the killing may have been related to organised crime in the area. I put my face in my hands and thought, not for the first time, Holy shit, how did I get mixed up in this?

Patrick rang and said, "Can I pop around and see you later?"

"Of course you can. Have you come up with anything?"

"Maybe but let's not talk about it on the phone."

"OK, see you later."

I felt mildly irritated that Patrick was becoming paranoid about people listening in to phone calls. Was it all the fuss about the recent phone hacking scandals and the 'Big Brother' listening devices apparently used by the government to thwart terrorism? Or did he think that somehow Leon might have bugged his phone? Either way I'd have to wait a bit longer to hear whatever it was he'd come up with.

*

I barely let him get through the door before asking what his big idea was.

"I haven't really got anything yet but I thought we could try a bit of brainstorming and see what we come up with."

I was disappointed that Patrick was reducing my problem to some kind of project management exercise. But then that was how we'd been trained to deal with business problems so why not apply the technique to personal problems too?

Patrick had brought his briefcase and I half expected him to pull out a massive whiteboard and some marker pens, but instead he just pulled out a writing pad and pen and started drawing four quadrants in which he wrote: 'strengths', 'weaknesses', 'opportunities', 'threats'. When he'd done that he looked up expectantly, his pen poised.

"Let's start with the easy one," I said, deciding to play along, at least for a while. "Threats – I could get killed, I could get maimed, I could go to jail."

Patrick wrote them all down and sucked the end of his pen thoughtfully, then, speaking as he wrote it down he added, "Family, loved ones could get hurt."

"Do you think he might hurt Ella?" Even as I said it, I knew Leon would stop at nothing and felt a chill as I remembered how Leon apparently 'bumped into her' in France. I was convinced that was no coincidence.

"Only to get to you," Patrick replied.

"OK. Let's move onto 'Weaknesses'." I wanted to change the subject. "Are we talking his weaknesses, or mine?"

"Let's focus on yours. His weaknesses may come under the heading 'Opportunities'."

"I scare easily, I'm naive, particularly about criminal matters."

"Anything else?"

"I get very little notice that a job is going down and I'm told even less about what's actually going to happen. I don't usually know until we get wherever it is we're going. Sometimes I don't even know what's happening even then!"

Patrick wrote this all down and then his pen hovered over the 'Opportunities' quadrant and he wrote: 'Working as an insider gives an opportunity to gain their trust'.

I nodded. "I think they do trust me to an extent; they're just naturally cautious."

"Do they think you're naive?"

"Yes, almost certainly."

Under 'Strengths' Patrick wrote 'they underestimate us'.

When I saw Patrick had written 'us' I felt a surge of emotion: I wasn't in this alone anymore. I was so glad I'd confided in Patrick.

We played around with the four quadrants for a while longer until the ideas began to dry up.

Then Patrick asked, "Have you thought of going to the police?"

"What could I tell them?"

"Well, quite a lot I would have thought – you know where the bodies are buried for a start. You also know the whereabouts of a murder weapon, and you have some advance notice when jobs or deals are about to happen. Maybe they could set something up in advance and catch them in the act?"

I began dismissing each suggestion in turn. "One," I said, "I know where the bodies are but not who actually killed them and Leon was nowhere near and probably, knowing him as I do, he'll have a watertight alibi while we were burying them. Two, the murder weapon I disposed of was used against one of Leon's own men so I don't see how that would help implicate Leon. And finally, three, even if I had more notice and knew what was going to happen and where, Leon never comes near the actual deals. He's no fool."

Patrick sighed with frustration.

"And if I did turn police informant and help put him behind bars, then Ella and I, and probably Katrina, would have to disappear into some kind of police protection programme because you can bet your life Leon would have me hunted down and killed, even if it was from prison. I'd never have another day's rest without constantly looking over my shoulder. I'm not sure I could live like that!"

"OK, here's an idea," Patrick said, visibly brightening. "We have to find a way of entrapping Leon so he ends up being sent down for a long time without him ever knowing it was you who shopped him!"

I felt tired and deflated. "You're right, but I think that's going to be a lot easier said than done."

"Well at least we have a starting point," Patrick said, clearly trying to keep me positive. "Let's stop now and sleep on it and something will occur to us, I'm sure."

That night I slept very badly again, tossing and turning

and hitting mental brick walls down every road I travelled.

The next day, with nothing to do until evening when I was due to meet Ella. I couldn't face moping around the flat all day and, as the sun was shining, decided to go for a long walk up a mountain somewhere. The Brecon Beacons were only about an hour away, or better still, the Black Mountains.

I drove to Hay-on-Wye, bought some sandwiches and had a flask of tea made for me in a cafe. Then I set off to wander aimlessly around the hills overlooking the town. I quite deliberately left my mobile phones in the van deciding that for the next couple of hours I'd be incommunicado. When I returned about four o'clock I felt the most relaxed I'd been for ages and pleasantly physically tired rather than emotionally shattered. I still hadn't found any solutions though.

I felt a twinge of concern when I saw two missed calls from Ella. I hoped she wasn't going to cancel and immediately rang her back.

"Hi Lovely, I see you've been trying to get hold of me?"

"Where have you been? I tried twice."

"I'm in Hay-on-Wye and the… errr… signal isn't so good here."

"I just wanted to check we're still on for tonight," she said. "Where are you taking me?"

Relief flooded through me. "We're definitely still on," I said, "and I'll take you wherever you want to go."

"How about that new Italian in town, you know, the one with the fake flame lamps burning outside. It's supposed to be really good there."

"Sure, why not? I'll pick you up about seven if you like and make sure you bring your holiday photos."

"They're all on my phone, silly," she said, sounding delighted all the same. "But can I meet you there Dad? I'm not at home, I'm staying with a friend."

"Oh? Everything all right?"

"Yeah, I'll tell you when I see you later. 'Bye for now."

She sounded a bit troubled and cagey when she said she was staying with a friend. I hoped she hadn't fallen out with her mother. They did have the occasional mother/teenage daughter type rows and I wondered how they'd cope without me there to referee.

After a shower and a shave I arrived at the restaurant early and then waited and waited for Ella to show. I must've glanced at my watch about fourteen times as I waited at the bar with a soft drink. I was seated just inside the entrance where we'd agreed to meet and she was half an hour late. It was beginning to worry me. It wasn't like her to be late and not to at least ring to warn me. When I wasn't checking my watch I was looking at the phone, checking there was a signal – all five bars of signal strength were present. I began to imagine the worst; maybe she'd been knocked over or had some kind of accident. It crossed my mind that Leon had snatched her as some kind of insurance against me cooperating tonight but that was ridiculous, he had no reason to suspect I wouldn't be there. I told myself to stop being so paranoid.

After another fifteen minutes, I tried her mobile phone but it went straight to voicemail. I was on the point of ringing the local hospital's accident and emergency department when the restaurant door opened and in she walked, removing her hat and shaking her long red hair. She was beautiful, no doubt about it, and the Italian waiters fought almost comically to be first to take her coat.

Her smile was radiant. "Hi Dad, sorry I'm late."

"I was worried about you, I tried to ring you."

"My battery's low so I left it at home on charge."

The father in me resisted an urge to tell her she should always carry it with her when she was out at night.

"Well, you're here now that's the main thing," I said, giving her a big hug. "Let's go and order, I'm starving!"

"So, if you've left your phone behind does that mean I don't get to see any photos?" I asked.

She produced an iPod from her bag with a flourish and

said, "You don't get let off that easily; I transferred them onto this!"

There were ninety-seven photos, most of which were dark grainy photos of her and her friends drinking in different bars. These were interspersed with some rather unflattering photographs of their untidy holiday flat and friends caught in compromising poses whilst asleep. There were a couple of nice views taken from their balcony but I had to admit that Ella's skills lay in areas other than photography. My mood changed abruptly when a photo of Leon appeared. He had his hands on Ella's shoulders and his eyes were staring straight at the camera. To me there was something sinister in his grin that reminded me of a wolf. I shivered so much at the sight of him that Ella asked me if I was cold.

"Your friend Leon was really nice to us," she said. "He even offered to let us all stay a few days at his vineyard but some of the others had different plans."

"How on earth did you meet?" I asked.

"We were having coffee on a pavement cafe and he came up to us and asked if I was your daughter – said he recognised me from a photo on your desk. That's so cute, Dad, I never realised you kept a photo of me at work."

Our conversation about the holiday lasted throughout the starter and main course. Then I gently probed as to why Ella was staying with a friend and not at home. It was just as I thought; she and Katrina had had a big row.

"I'm eighteen in a couple of months," Ella protested, "an adult, and she still treats me like I'm a child!"

I let out a long slow breath. It sounded like the same old argument that bubbled to the surface every few months and probably repeated itself in every household that held a teenager on the brink of adulthood. It was something and nothing and I felt sure it would all blow over in a couple of days, or as soon as Ella started missing home comforts.

Ella's next remark did concern me however.

"And I don't much like the way Tim treats me," she said.

She had my full attention now.

"Why what do you mean? How is he treating you?"

"No, nothing like that," Ella said, as if reading my mind. "It's just that he seems to think he can order me around in my own home and he's so disapproving of my friends. I hate the way he paws Mum. Whenever I'm around, he seems to be all over her like a rash. It's almost as if he's trying to prove to me that he loves her more than you did. I hate the prick!"

"There's no need for language like that!" I said, even though I was thinking exactly the same thought.

"Well he is one! I really don't know what Mum sees in him."

I felt at a loss what to say next. I certainly had no idea what Katrina saw in Tim either, but I didn't really want to get into that with my daughter.

"I'm sorry I rang you that time in the middle of the night, Dad," Ella looked sheepish. "I was a bit drunk and feeling sorry for myself. I just wanted you two to get back together again and I felt sad that you were splitting up. And I blame myself, Dad. Maybe if Mum and I hadn't had so many rows then you and she might have been happier together because I know they sometimes caused arguments between you two as well."

I reached across the table and took her warm hands in mine. She was looking down at her plate so I gently reached across and tilted her chin up until she looked at me and then said, "It isn't your fault in any way Ella so you really mustn't blame yourself. I realise now that your Mum and I were growing apart and finding we had little left in common."

I didn't believe what I was telling her about us growing apart, but it had to be said for her sake because one thing was for sure in my mind and that was that the beautiful young woman sitting opposite me was in no way at fault.

"I'm pretty certain we won't be getting back together though Ella, I think too much has happened and it would never be the same again between us. We'll probably be happier apart. But just because we've stopped loving each other doesn't mean for one second that either one of us has stopped loving you, or that we ever will. We'll both always be there for you, you do know that don't you, love?"

Ella nodded but her eyes were filled.

"So who's this friend you're staying with? Anyone I know?"

"Chloe, but don't tell Mum!"

"Do you mean she doesn't know where you are?"

Ella nodded guiltily.

"Listen, love, you mustn't be too hard on her, she'll be worried sick about you if she doesn't even know where you are. At least tell her you're with a friend and safe."

"OK Dad, I'll tell her."

I tried to glance at my watch without her noticing but she spotted me.

"Am I boring you now?" she said, only half joking.

"No, of course you're not; I'm never bored in your company."

It was quarter to eleven and I didn't want to tell her I had to be somewhere at eleven thirty as that would involve explanations and probably lies and I hated the thought of lying to her.

"It's OK," she said, yawning. "I'm pretty tired myself and just about ready to hit the sack."

"Come on then, I'll run you around to Chloe's place."

"I can walk, it's not far."

"At this time of night? No way! I won't hear of it; come on."

I dropped her outside Chloe's parent's house, wondering what they thought about the sleepover arrangements and how much they knew about Katrina and myself. I'd only met them a couple of times, usually at school parent events, and they seemed nice enough.

Robert Darke

CHAPTER TWENTY-THREE

I drove straight to the lock-up and arrived about ten minutes early to find the place in complete darkness. Although I had a key, I wasn't sure whether or not to go in and see what was in there waiting to be loaded. I decided to wait because I didn't want to be caught snooping and I had a feeling Winsome had forgotten he'd given me a key. And who knows when or if it may come in handy that it remained that way.

Winsome and Mike turned up fifteen minutes later. They didn't open the garage, they just came straight over to the van. Mike was carrying a briefcase and Winsome had a set of number plates under his arm.

"Don't worry, they're clean," he said to me, as I jumped out of the cab to greet them.

I looked at the plates and tried to memorise the number in case I was routinely stopped by the police. The plates looked a bit wet, as though they were coated with something.

I ran a finger across the surface.

"They got some kinda special coating supposed to stop speed cameras from reading the number," Winsome explained. "Apparently it reflects the flash right back at the camera."

"Does it work?" I thought it seemed unlikely.

"Dunno, but I suggest you don't test it just in case."

"So are we going to load this van, or what?" I was irritated by their lateness.

Winsome made no move towards the garage, instead he just said, "Nope, tonight we're buying, not selling."

Mike had already climbed into the cab with his briefcase which I now assumed must be full of money.

"What are we buying?" I asked.

"About a thousand kilos of pure heroin straight out of Afghanistan," Winsome said.

"What?!"

Winsome found that funny; "For Christ sake, Marty, I told you Leon doesn't deal in drugs so just relax!"

"So what is it we're buying?" I persisted.

"Look, what difference does it make to you, all you gotta do is drive the bloody van!"

"I like to know what it is I'm getting into, that's all. Why all the bloody secrecy every time there's a job? Don't you trust me yet? I'm sick of always being kept in the dark!"

"OK, no need to get all emotional on us," Winsome growled. "We're gonna buy thirty grand's worth of knocked-off iPads with a wholesale market value of twice that and we've already found a trader who we can offload them to at a tidy profit. So tonight we take delivery of goods and take 'em back to the lock up and tomorrow night we shift 'em on out to the wholesaler. Happy now?"

"I've got no deliveries to make tomorrow, why can't we save a bit of time and just leave them on the van?"

"Are you mad? D'ya think I'm gonna risk leaving stuff with a retail value of one hundred grand in the back of your van overnight and all day – and in that shit area where you live?"

I couldn't really argue with that, especially as the van had already been broken into once.

"Fair enough," I said, sullenly climbing into the driver's seat. "Where to?"

"Birmingham."

"But that's two hours away!"

"So stop with all the chatter and get bloody driving, will you?"

We all fell into an uneasy silence. Winsome put the radio on and tuned it to some late night jazz programme with a whispering disc jockey that threatened to put me to sleep. There was a palpable tension in the air which was unsettling as I'd never seen my two partners in crime this subdued.

In the end, I had to know why. "So tell me a bit about what we're going into tonight. Because, if you don't mind me saying, you both seem a bit quiet."

Winsome asked, "Have you ever heard of the Yardies, Marty?"

"I seem to remember reading about them in the newspapers a few years back. Aren't they Jamaican gangsters who coined that name because they came from the government yards in Trenchtown? Weren't they were responsible for a lot of gun crime in London?"

"Yer right, and not just London. They spread to other cities too and the Birmingham bunch caused a lot of problems with the local Aggi Crew when they arrived. Cor, remember that Mike? They put armed coppers on the street to stop the buggers slaughtering each other."

Mike nodded. "Too right I remember," he agreed, "the bastards we were dealing with were a right bunch of crack heads. Mad as hatters – never knew what they were going to do next!"

"Are you telling me we're doing this deal tonight with a gang of Yardies?"

"Yer got it in one," Winsome said. "Why Leon wants to deal with 'em is beyond me but I suppose it's a lucrative deal if we can just pull it off without incident."

I could feel my palms wet and slippery on the driving

wheel. Suddenly, I felt wide awake.

"What we gotta watch is for the whites of their eyes," Mike said. "If they're high on drugs the eyes will give them away and we get the fuck out of there before the shooting starts."

"They've calmed down a lot now," Winsome added. "They had to become more professional; you can't operate any kind of business if the police are all over you. Mind you, they're certain to be tooled up but then so are we and they'll know that too. And our money is a whole lot more use to them than a van load of iPads, so we should be OK."

"Oh bloody Hell!" I pulled the van into a lay-by and quickly ran around to the side and hankered down. Only just getting my pants down in time. When I'd finished I called for Mike to throw me the roll of toilet paper I'd taken to keeping in the glove box.

When I climbed sheepishly back into the driver's seat Winsome said, "Jesus, there was no need to shit yerself! I think we'd better drive with the windows open for a bit."

As they reached the outskirts of the city, Winsome said, "OK guys, this is how I see us playing it tonight. When we arrive you stay behind the wheel, Marty, and keep the engine running. Mike and I will get out, show them the money and our guns. Once they've seen that they'll know we mean business and there ain't no reason why they shouldn't start loading the gear into the van. I want you to stay in the van at all times Marty and, as before, if there's any sign of trouble just drive off. Mike and I can look after ourselves. Got it?"

"Yes," I said. I didn't like the sound of it one bit but at least I didn't have to get out of the van and help load the boxes.

"Once the van is loaded we hand over the money and get the fuck out of there. That handover is the most dangerous time, Marty, cos that's when they might decide to keep the money and take back the goods. So keep the van in gear and yer foot on the clutch ready to drive away. And like I said, don't worry about Mike and me."

I looked earnestly at Winsome. "This had better not be another of your bloody hoaxes," I said.

"Straight up this is for real, Marty, on my mother's grave."

*

When we reached the venue, Winsome cursed quietly, "This place sucks," he said. "Anyone could be watching from these surrounding buildings, police, rival gangs. What were the idiots thinking of choosing here?"

I drove around the site but Winsome was right – it was a pointless exercise because there were just too many derelict buildings. The satnav coordinates we'd been given took us to a dead end and Mike suggested we turn the van around ready for a quick getaway.

We sat nervously waiting. A black Mercedes with the windows down and loud rap music blaring drove up to and stopped in front of the van. It was impossible in the glare of the headlights to see how many of them were in the car.

They seemed to wait ages before three men got out, all of them brandishing guns.

Winsome made no attempt to get out to meet them, instead he just wound the window down a fraction so they could speak.

A big guy sauntered up to the window and said, "You got the bread?"

Winsome immediately replied, "You got the goods?"

The man grinned at him. "We gotta van just around the corner, just waiting for the call, but he don't get no call 'till we see the money."

Winsome nodded to Mike who pulled the briefcase from the floor onto his lap. He opened the lid and tilted the contents towards the waiting Yardie.

The man took a mobile phone from his pocket and the conversation was short and to the point. "OK, Bro, game on!"

He grinned again and put his hand out for the briefcase of money but Winsome held up his hand. "Not until we have the goods safely loaded in the van," he said.

We didn't have long to wait before the headlights of a transit van bobbed along the deserted roads at some speed. More rap music was blaring from the van as it pulled up alongside our van, effectively blocking us in as the black Merc was still parked in front of him. I looked to Winsome for guidance.

"Don't worry Marty," he said. "I'll get 'em to pull it forward a bit to make it easier to offload the boxes onto our van. That should give us a gap to squeeze through if things kick off. And remember, if they do, drive off and find somewhere safe to wait for us and make sure you're not followed!"

"OK," I said. My underarms were uncomfortably damp and I could feel my stomach muscles cramping again. I prayed I could hold out.

Three more Yardies piled out of the van which meant we were outnumbered two to one. At least the new guys were not waving guns around, but that didn't mean they weren't tucked away in their belts somewhere.

Their leader told them to cut the music. Mike and Winsome jumped out and opened the back of the van.

I heard Winsome's saying, "Come on guys move the bloody van forward a bit, we don't wanna cart these boxes further than we have to."

Their van jerked forward and I sighed with relief as a gap opened just as Winsome had planned. The briefcase containing the money remained on the passenger seat and I looked at it nervously.

Mike picked a box at random for inspection and asked them to open it. He took out a slimmer box with Apple branding on it and opened that too. Inside was a pristine looking iPad still in protective cellophane. Mike pressed a button and a moment later the screen sparked into life.

"Looks OK to me," he said.

They started shifting all the other boxes from one van to the other and when they were all finally loaded Winsome came back for the briefcase and quietly urged, "Be ready to go, Marty."

I was ready, my fingers tapping impatiently on the wheel. I heard voices being raised behind and checked the wing mirrors but the only person I could see was one of the guys who had arrived in the second van. The man looked restless and sort of danced on the spot like he was nervous. I was so intent on watching him that I didn't see Winstone and Mike in my other wing mirror coming along the side of the van. When they opened the door I jumped like hell.

Winsome said, "OK we've got the goods so let's not hang about. I think something is going down between those two posses don't you, Mike?"

"Yeah, I didn't like the way that second crew were looking around all the time checking the surroundings." Mike added. No sooner had he finished the sentence, than some sort of commotion started up behind the van. Mike looked at me hard and said, "Well come on! If you can get through that gap then let's get the fuck out of here!"

I spun the wheel and jerked out with just an inch to spare between the Mercedes and the other van. Someone banged the side of the van. I straightened her up and floored the accelerator. The clutch screamed and the wheels spun and screeched. As we roared away down the lane I saw a flash of flame in my wing mirror and heard a loud bang.

I had no idea if someone had fired at us but I had no intention of waiting to find out. As we turned a corner more gunfire sounded behind us.

"My gut feeling was right again," Winsome said. "Reckon we got outta there just in time."

It was 5:00am by the time we'd unloaded the van and I finally turned the key in my own front door. I was so exhausted that I didn't wake up until one o'clock that afternoon. I made myself a strong coffee and turned on the TV for the news just in time to hear the newsreader saying; "We're just getting news in of a shooting incident in Birmingham. Police say a young man was shot dead in the early hours of this morning on an industrial estate on the outskirts of Birmingham. The man, who has not been named, was believed to have come from Kingston, Jamaica. One eye witness is said to have seen a white van speeding away from the scene. *Shit!*" Police believe the killing may have been gang related and are appealing for witnesses who may have seen something to come forward.

By six o'clock they'd named the deceased man as Archibald Winston Moke (aged 19), who left behind a wife and baby daughter. But there were no further developments other than a fresh appeal for anyone seeing anything suspicious to dial the Crime Stoppers number. Much to my relief, there was no further mention of a white van speeding away. Thank goodness Winsome had had the foresight to switch number plates. Even if we had been caught on camera, they'd not have any direct link back to me.

CHAPTER TWENTY-FOUR

That evening Patrick and I sat gloomily supping beers at a quiet table in the corner of the Rose and Crown. So far, he hadn't come up with anything tangible that would help me out of this predicament. I couldn't help feeling a little disappointed although I could hardly blame my friend when I had no ideas either.

"There must be something we can do." I hadn't realised I'd spoken the thought aloud.

Patrick frowned and said, "Somehow we need to get him caught without there being any suspicion in his mind that you were instrumental in his downfall."

The germ of an idea formed in my mind.

"So far he's done all of his dealings on a cash basis and they are not the sort of amounts he would keep under his mattress – we both know what a shrewd investor he is. There's no way he would leave large sums of money around not earning interest for him. But last night we handed over a briefcase with forty grand inside."

Patrick looked at me. "How does that help us?" he asked.

"I get virtually no warning of what's going on until the very last minute – I don't think they trust me enough yet and besides they're very cautious in the way they operate - but if his money is held in interest-bearing accounts then he probably has to give at least three days notice of withdrawal." I looked at Patrick. "If you monitored his accounts for large withdrawals then that would give us more warning and therefore more time to set something up."

Patrick looked uncertain. "You're asking me to break the rules," he said. "That prick Pierce would sack me for sure if I'm caught!"

"Not if Leon asked you to monitor his accounts for him to ensure he is always getting the best rates."

"Well he hasn't done that yet, not in all the time we've known him!"

Patrick's lack of understanding was starting to irk me. I decided to spell it out for him. "But no one has ever suggested it to him – if you were to offer to monitor his accounts to ensure he was always on the best rate he certainly wouldn't say no, would he? And you don't have to tell Pierce the suggestion came from you – just get Leon to sign an authorisation and you're covered!"

"But he may not come in for months," Patrick persisted stubbornly.

"Oh, he'll be in within a few days. Trust me! He's just done a deal that will net him an enormous profit and he'll be in to deposit the proceeds in no time at all."

"OK, I'll try suggesting it to him, but I still don't really see how a few extra days notice is going to help us to set him up."

"Leave that to me," I said, "I'll think of something."

*

The following morning at nine o'clock Leon called at the flat.

I let him in with mixed feelings, remembering the last time he was there I'd been slapped and beaten to the ground. I wasn't expecting an apology but, this morning at least, he seemed to be in high spirits.

"I hear you did well the other night," he said, "stayed calm under pressure and got the hell out of there before the shooting started. Well done, here's a little bonus for you."

He took a white envelope out of his pocket and handed it to me. It felt a good weight and I couldn't help thinking that I'd earned almost as much from Leon's bonuses as I had in salary. Who says crime doesn't pay? I'd pretty much decided that, however much was in the envelope, I'd try and donate it anonymously to the widow and child of that dead Yardie – maybe the kid could find a better way to live than his dad had.

"Thanks, Leon, it's much appreciated," I said.

"Tell me something, Martin," Leon said, his eyes boring into me. "That gun you disposed of for me the other day. Is there any chance you could retrieve it?"

I studied Leon's face looking for any sign that he had somehow learned that I'd hidden the gun I was asked to destroy. There was nothing in that poker face of his to be read.

I hoped my own face was equally impassive as I replied, "Not unless you want to hire some frogmen to drag the River Usk!"

Leon looked pleased and I think maybe I'd just escaped another beating for not following orders. My tension eased a little.

"Ah well," Leon said, "guess I'll just have to get another one then."

"What for?" I asked. It was out before I'd even given it a thought and I instantly regretted asking.

Leon shot me a look but his good mood seemed to prevail. "Something I may need to deal with," he said. "Tell me, Martin, have you ever killed anyone?"

"Never!"

"You've been very loyal to me so far, Martin. If I were to test that loyalty further by asking you to kill someone for me what would you do?"

I felt light headed and held onto the back of the chair to stop myself swaying.

"I er... I'm not... well, I mean..." I stammered, clutching my other hand to his stomach.

Leon roared with laughter, "It's OK Martin, relax, I'm only kidding, I know you couldn't kill anyone, your eyes tell me that – you simply don't have it in you."

I felt my shoulders sag with relief, trying to put on a brave face as I said, "You had me going there for a minute!"

"I know, you went white; I thought you were going to faint for a minute!" He dabbed at his laughter tears with a handkerchief. "I'm sorry I couldn't resist winding you up, it's true what Winsome says about you – you fall for it every time!"

"In that case, I might just kill him next time I see him!"

Leon's smile disappeared then as fast as the sun going behind a cloud. "Seriously though my friend, I may need you to do a bit more cleaning up for me – another moonlight garden landscaping job – you up for that?"

"Sure," I said, knowing I had no other option but to agree.

"Good man," Leon nodded with satisfaction as he made to leave, "and get rid of those new false number plates from the Birmingham job as they may be compromised."

"Winsome's already disposed of them."

"Excellent," Leon said, and he left, closing the door silently behind him. As expected, there was no further mention of my resignation.

I slumped into a chair but soon had to get up again as my stomach started its familiar cramping. Twenty minutes later, I decided I really must see a doctor.

I thought about what Leon had just said and how I might use it against him. Was he really planning a murder? Or was this another elaborate hoax to test my metal. I really wasn't sure. There was nothing of any real value, without a who, what, why, how, when, and where I couldn't see the police being very interested without those answers. I rang the doctor but was told all that day's appointments were gone and I have to wait until tomorrow.

I went for a coffee in Beth's Café.

The cafe was quiet and Beth greeted me enthusiastically and joined me with a cup of her own.

"How are you doing?" she asked.

"Surviving," was all I said. I took a sip of the hot coffee and immediately my hand went to my stomach.

Beth noticed and said, "Are you OK?"

"Sorry, bowels have been playing up a bit – I'm seeing a doctor tomorrow."

"You've been under a lot of stress lately: losing your job, going through a divorce, moving out, starting your own business. These things all take their toll. I don't suppose working for Leon is exactly relaxing either."

I looked into her deep brown eyes. "You're right there," I said. "I wish I'd never taken him up on his damn job offer but it's too late now."

Her eyes flashed, "What do you mean too late?"

"I mean..." I hesitated, wondering how much I could tell her. She waited patiently for an answer. She was the kind of woman one could trust and who could keep a secret and God knows I felt the need to talk to someone. "I mean I'm already in too deep with him for him to easily let me go – I know too much about his affairs."

A brief, almost cynical smile flickered across Beth's lips. "Affairs? Interesting choice of word. Does he have many affairs?" she asked.

"I meant business affairs."

"I'm sorry, I was being a bit facetious. Martin, if I tell you something, can I trust you not to breathe a word of it to anyone else?"

"Yes, of course you can," I said, wondering what was coming next.

"I once had an affair with Leon, and I don't mean a business affair either. It was a long time ago now, water under the bridge. The reason I'm telling you is so that you'll understand that I too know a lot more than most about Leon Cooper and what he is capable of doing to get his way."

I was stunned by this news. A woman came into the cafe and Beth got up to serve her. To be honest, I was glad of the opportunity to absorb what this meant. Here was someone who seemed to know all about Leon and yet had survived apparently unscathed, to all appearances at least. That knowledge gave me hope that maybe there was some way out for me too.

Beth returned and sat back opposite me. She was about to say something when another customer came in. She smiled and as she rose said, "We can't talk here; it's too public. Why don't you come around to my place tonight?"

She wrote her address on a paper serviette. "Come about eight o'clock," she said.

It was only afterwards, when I thought about it I realised that going to her home was moving our relationship up a notch and suddenly I felt a little unsure of myself.

*

I had time to kill and wandered aimlessly around the shops in Albany Road and Wellfield Road. I walked past my old bank branch and wondered about going in and saying hello but decided it'd be too embarrassing, especially if I bumped into that idiot Pierce, so I walked past. Glancing through the glass doors, I caught sight of Patrick with a client. He seemed to be staring out into space with a bored look on his face and gave no indication that he'd seen me. Although it had been only a few months, the world of banking already seemed like a lifetime ago now. I was surprised to realise how much I missed it – the daily routine, the banter, the certainty of what I was supposed to be doing. How my life had changed.

Five minutes later Patrick rang my mobile.

"Was that you I just saw walking past?"

So he had seen me.

"Yes."

"You should have popped in, said hello."

"I thought about it, but... Well you know..."

"I wanted to see you anyway – have you got time to meet for lunch, say about twelve?"

I glanced at my watch, it meant me hanging around for the best part of an hour.

"I've got some news about our mutual friend," Patrick said.

That clinched it. "Great," I said, "see you later."

*

We found seats in a corner of a newly-opened wine bar. Patrick was trying his hardest to eat a baguette without squeezing egg mayo out all over his shirt. I glanced around making sure we couldn't be overheard and asked, "So what's this news then?"

Patrick also glanced nervously around the neighbouring tables and I couldn't help thinking that if we kept behaving like a couple of amateur spies we'd actually draw attention to ourselves.

"I was thinking about what you said about Leon always paying bonuses in cash and checked his accounts for cash withdrawals. As you suspected, two days before you went to Birmingham, he withdrew significant sums of money from four different savings accounts.

"Then I checked further back and there were similar patterns before each of the other jobs you mentioned – so even though he doesn't tell you until hours before, if I monitor his account then we should get a couple of days notice that something is going down even if we don't know what!"

"That's brilliant Patrick, well done!"

I thought for a moment then added, "The question is will that be sufficient evidence to tie him into the job – I mean he never actually comes to any of these things and I wouldn't mind betting he makes sure he has a water-tight alibi on the nights in question."

Patrick looked glum. "It is a bit circumstantial," he agreed, "but it's a start at least."

"I'm wondering whether to talk to that detective inspector," I said. "He'll have a much better idea of what kind of evidence is permissible in court and the rules that need to be followed."

"Yes, but isn't that taking a hell of a chance? Once the police know you're involved there'll be no turning back you know."

"I know but I'm pretty certain he already suspects me of being involved and who knows, the net may already be tightening around Leon – at least if I'm cooperating I might manage to stay on the outside of it when it comes about."

"Can you trust him? I mean don't a lot of these gangster types have coppers taking backhanders to warn them of investigations? You can't afford to make any mistakes, Martin, we know this guy is a real player and the more people who know what we're planning the greater the danger of him finding us out and murdering us both!"

For the first time I noticed a slight tremble in Patrick's hand as he raised his wine glass to his lips. "I'll keep your name out of it, I promise, Patrick. I don't want to place you in danger – this is my mess and not of your doing."

"All the same, it was my choice to help so I am involved and I want to nail this bloke as much as you do."

He licked the remainder of his egg mayonnaise baguette off his fingers and we finished our drinks in silence.

CHAPTER TWENTY-FIVE

Back at the flat I showered and shaved and ironed a shirt. I felt nervous about going to Beth's house later. Should I buy flowers? Or would that seem too much like a first date? Was it a first date? Of course not, but it felt like one and I found myself wishing it was. All she wanted was somewhere private to talk, I kept telling myself. If I turned up wearing aftershave and bearing flowers it could be horribly embarrassing. The truth was I didn't have a clue what to do; after all, I'd not been dating for over thirty years. *And you're not dating now!* I had to keep reminding myself.

In the end, I put on my best pair of jeans and an open neck shirt, and took a bottle of wine. Her house was a large detached house in a tree-lined avenue near Roath Park Lake. The lawns were neat and tidy with well kept flower borders and not a weed in sight. I'd assumed she lived alone but it suddenly occurred to me she may well be in a relationship – just because she wore no ring it meant nothing.

An old-fashioned portico sheltered the front door and I gathered myself before reaching for the bell push with a trembling hand. I heard a melodic chime and saw her outline approaching through the stained glass. I wiped my sweaty palm on my jeans ready to shake her hand. When she opened the door, she took my breath away – I hardly recognised her. I was used to seeing her in her cafe overalls and apron but now she wore a delicate lilac dress with a bold floral pattern that ended just below her knees, revealing shapely calves. She had make-up on too, another first, and her luxuriant brown hair fell loose over her shoulders instead of scraped back into a ponytail with a blue chef's hat on top.

It was a transformation. I'd always found her attractive but now I saw that she was beautiful.

Shaking her hand suddenly seemed awkward and inappropriate so I just extended the hand holding the wine bottle and said, "I thought I'd bring us something to drink."

It sounded lame, even as I spoke the words, but Beth just raised an eyebrow for the briefest of moments and then took the bottle and in the same easy motion went up on tiptoe and pecked me affectionately on the cheek.

"I'm so glad you could come," she said, sounding genuinely pleased to see me. "Let's go in here."

She guided me from the wide entrance hall into a room that faced the rear of the house with patio doors looking out onto the back garden which was every bit as neat and tidy as the front, but with an even more spectacular display of flowers.

"Wow," I said. "Where do you find the time to garden?"

"I don't! My 71-year-old mother does it all; well she has a man in to help her do the heavy stuff. She moved into a sheltered flat just round the corner and misses her garden so I asked her to look after mine – we share it – except sometimes I feel she does all the work and I get all the pleasure."

I sat on a sofa and she said, "I'll go and open this wine and fetch us some glasses."

On impulse, I took both my own and the works mobile phones and switched them both off. I didn't want anything to disturb our evening.

"So, let's talk about our mutual acquaintance Leon Cooper," Beth said when she returned. She set two glasses on the table and poured out a generous quantity. I'd expected her to sit opposite but instead she settled on the sofa right next to me. I could smell her perfume and now wished I'd put on some aftershave.

"You start," I said.

"OK. I met Leon about eight years ago at a business function; I can't even remember what it was now, some kind of fund-raising event I think. We were on the same table sitting next to each other and just seemed to hit it off. We danced and then well, we'd both had a bit to drink and he suggested neither of us should drive home so he booked a double room in the hotel hosting the function.

"I knew he was married - he never tried to hide it. At the dinner table he had even shown me photos of his daughter. He spun me the usual cliché about his wife not understanding him and to be honest I didn't much care. I was coming out of a messy divorce and just felt plain lonely." She hesitated. "I sound like a tramp don't I?"

I shook my head. "Right now, I know all about the loneliness of going through a divorce."

Our eyes met briefly and Beth said, "Of course you do; I'm sorry. Anyway, we saw each other afterwards, always in secret, and I think we both believed briefly we were in love. He promised to leave his wife but couldn't face the upset it would cause his daughter. Gradually I think we both realised it was just an infatuation and in the end he offered to buy me off by lending me the money to buy the cafe at zero interest, for a twenty percent share of the business."

"Does he still own that share?"

Beth shook her head. "I bought him out a couple of years ago so he has no interest in my business now. I prefer it that way."

We fell into silence but it was a companionable pause where we both sat looking at the garden. The evening was quiet and still and warm enough for her to leave the patio doors open.

After a while, Beth quietly continued her story. "He used to confide in me about how he made money; I think he liked to brag about it. I knew some, well, most of his dealings even back then were criminal, fencing stolen goods, that kind of thing. And he could be pretty ruthless with anyone who got in his way. He never admitted killing anyone to me but I'm quite sure he was capable of it, might even enjoy it. He has quite a cruel vindictive streak but, for some reason, it never surfaced when he was with me. He was kind to me and I think he trusted me. We remain on friendly terms even to this day but I don't see much of him anymore and I think, and maybe you can confirm this, Martin, he's now even more deeply immersed in criminal activities."

I nodded. "I think maybe you got out just in time. He can be violent and quick-tempered, which makes him dangerously unpredictable.

"I first got to know him when he came into the bank for investment advice. He is a very wealthy man – a millionaire and I received a lot of kudos when he transferred his current and savings accounts to our bank. At first I gave him straightforward investment advice but, gradually, he quizzed me about money laundering and how to stay under the radar. That should have rung alarm bells but because he was by far my best client, and I didn't want to lose him, I ignored the signs. It didn't feel like I was doing much wrong and it seemed a small price to pay to keep his accounts with us.

"Then, well you know the rest: I got made redundant, bought a van and went freelance. It turns out that the guy who beat me up worked for Leon and was 'protecting his interests'. At the time, I thought it was just coincidence when I delivered that buffet to Leon's home. Except the more I think about it I can't help believing that Leon was sat in the back of that 4x4 watching the whole beating from behind the blacked out windows. I just had the sense someone was watching. I believe he had his sights on me for a while and the whole thing was an elaborate charade to get me working for him. And sadly it worked!"

Beth looked thoughtful. "He's certainly capable of that kind of forward planning and he usually gets what he wants. It would be typical of the way he operates too, making you beholden to him, like you owe him a big favour."

"Thing is Beth, he's had me doing all sorts of shady stuff which I fear I could go to jail for and I don't know what to do, or how to extricate myself."

She refreshed our glasses and sat next to me and, when she sat back down, rested her head on my shoulder. I could smell the scent of coconut shampoo in her hair. Her closeness was awakening something in me that hadn't stirred in quite a while but I didn't dare move for fear of breaking the spell.

After a while, Beth asked, "Have you thought of going to the police?"

"Yes, but what if Leon has a contact there? If he finds out I'd even approached them I'm sure he'd kill me."

"I know a copper who might be willing to help get Leon and I'm sure he's honest and trustworthy. If you like, I could approach him on your behalf, without telling him who you are, and see if he's interested. Do you want me to do that?"

"Would you?"

"Sure, I said I'd be happy to help."

"Thanks, Beth, I really appreciate your help." My arm had been resting across the back of the sofa behind her head and I allowed it to slip around her shoulders feeling as self-conscious as a teenager on a first date in a cinema. I gave her a friendly squeeze. "You're a good friend."

"Leon's an incredibly vain man, you know, always preening himself; he can't pass a mirror. I found he was very susceptible to flattery – maybe you could use that against him somehow."

Our conversation went around in a similar way to my discussions with Patrick and no real solution emerged. I could feel the wine going to my head. I hadn't given much thought when I brought the bottle as to how I'd get home as now I was well over the drink-drive limit.

"I can't drive after all this wine," I sighed. "I'd better order a taxi and pick the van up in the morning."

"I've got a better idea than that," Beth said turning her face up to mine. "Why don't you stay the night?"

I moved my face closer to hers and then our lips met and she put her arms around my neck. The kiss was tentative at first but then I felt her tongue burrowing into my mouth. It had been such a long time since I'd held a woman and the intensity of my reaction took my breath away. We clung onto each other and kissed several more times then Beth stood in front of me and, taking my hand in hers, led me silently up the stairs.

CHAPTER TWENTY-SIX

"Irritable Bowel Syndrome, known as IBS for short," the
doctor declared. "I must say you're taking this news very
well."

I'd scarcely been able to stop grinning all morning. All I
could think about was what happened last night.

"I'm sorry," I said. "What does that mean exactly?"

"It means you should take it easy, avoid stress wherever
possible and try to relax. IBS is not serious but it is
unpleasant, as you've already experienced. You must relax,
then you should soon start to feel better. Try and avoid
spicy foods and things like pulses and onions because they
can cause bloating and wind. If it doesn't settle down in a
couple of weeks then I'll refer you to a consultant for
further investigations Do you need a note for work?"

I shook my head. "I'm self-employed."

"Then you'll probably find it hard to give yourself time
off but that's what you must do if you want this to go away
and not get worse."

"I'll do my best," I said, already knowing that rest
wasn't an option just at the moment. But I did promise
myself a holiday when this was all over. Maybe I could
persuade Beth to come with me.

"Is that all?" the Doctor asked.

Oops! I'd drifted off again and could see from my reflection in the mirror behind the Doctor's desk that I had a silly grin on my face.

"Thanks, Doc," I said, reaching for the door handle.

I didn't much like the sound of being referred to a hospital specialist. My GP had just performed a rectal examination and I dreaded to think what the hospital might do. The memory of him snapping on his rubber gloves was enough to wipe the smile momentarily off my face for sure.

∗

When I returned to the flat, Winsome was waiting in my armchair and I jumped. "How the hell did you get in?" I demanded.

"Far too easily mate, you should get a proper five-lever mortise lock on that door! Not that that would have stopped me but it would have slowed me down at least!" Winsome said. "Anyway, where the hell have you been? We've been trying to reach you on the phone all night. Leon's been going spare. I told you to keep it on your person at all times!"

"I do," I said, fishing it out of my pocket and switching it on.

"You switched it off! I can't believe you! Don't you understand nothing, and I mean what can be more important than Leon or me calling you on that number? Nothing, that's what!"

"Sorry," I said. I'd actually forgotten it was off in all the excitement last night. Now the damn thing started pinging embarrassingly as messages and voice mails started coming through. "What was it you wanted?"

"We wanted you and your van for a job last night and now we've had to put it off until tonight – so you'd better be ready and not swanning off. Where were you anyway?" Winsome eyed him suspiciously.

I had to think quickly because I didn't want them

knowing I was with one of Leon's old flames. "I had to see a doctor about my bowels and there was a sign in his waiting room saying please switch all mobile phones off. I just forgot to put it back on afterwards."

"And what did he say?"

"Hmmm?"

"The doctor, what did he say?"

"I've got something called IBS and he said I should rest up for a couple of weeks."

Winsome snorted. "Good luck with persuading Leon you need time off," he sneered.

"The doctor offered to write me a note."

"Just make sure you and your sorry excuse for an arse pick me up at seven thirty tonight on the corner of Wilson Road, or Leon will no doubt see to it you get plenty of rest in a hospital bed. OK?"

I nodded, wondering what on earth they had lined up for that evening – it was too short notice to set-up any kind of trap and Patrick hadn't rung to say any money had been drawn out. Then I remembered my other, personal mobile was also switched off and cursed silently.

Winsome stood up to leave, saying, "Remember, half past seven, don't be late!"

I looked around the flat, it felt violated. I didn't think Winsome would stoop to stealing anything but I was horrified that he'd simply let himself in and would bet good money he had searched through my things looking for anything incriminating. I thanked my lucky stars that there was nothing to be found as I'd never been one to make notes or get my thoughts down on paper.

As soon as I was sure Winsome was out of the building, I switched my personal mobile on and within a few seconds it was beeping at me showing two missed calls, both from Patrick and a message on voicemail. The voicemail was also from Patrick, left the previous evening. I played it: "Call me as soon as you can." His voice sounded stressed. I dialled his number.

"Martin, where the hell have you been? I've been worried sick!"

"Sorry, mate, I switched my phone off yesterday evening and forgot to switch it back on. What's happened?"

"Our man drew some more money out yesterday in cash – not a massive amount, just three thousand."

"That ties in; he has another job lined up for me tonight so it's probably to pay us."

"Why didn't you tell me?"

"Because I was only told myself about five minutes ago, that's why."

"Do you know what the job is?"

"No idea, as usual. All I have is a place to pick people up and a time. Then I'll be told where we're going."

"Do they ever frisk you to see if you're wearing a wire?"

"No, they've never done that yet," I answered, wondering how they'd missed such a relatively simple check when they seemed so surveillance savvy in every other respect. Maybe they did trust me a little more than I gave them credit. "Why? Do you have something in mind?"

"If you were wearing a bug, I could listen in on the other end and then tip the police off anonymously when I heard where you were going."

I considered this. "It's an idea," I said, "but too short notice to do anything for tonight. Besides, if he has only drawn out a few grand then it can't be one of his big shady deals. Let's think about it and get the equipment and test it before we use it for real."

"OK, that sounds sensible. I'll surf the net and see what kind of equipment is available."

"Thanks, Patrick; I don't know what I'd do without your help."

"No problem, and Martin..."

"What?"

"...take care tonight."

I wondered what Leon had in store. If it wasn't a cash deal, what might it be? Not another body to dispose of, surely.

Just then Ella rang.

"Hi Dad, I was wondering if we could meet up for a meal tonight and have a chat."

"I've got a job to go to," I said. "Can it wait until tomorrow night?"

"OK," she said, not quite managing to hide her disappointment.

I wondered what was up. "Sorry, love, are you sure it can wait?"

"Yes, it's not like a problem, or anything, I'll see you tomorrow then."

We arranged to meet at the same restaurant as last time.

My thoughts returned to Beth and the wonderful night we'd shared. I was dying to call her and tell her how much I'd enjoyed himself but I kept putting it off because I felt like a tongue-tied teenager. My phone rang again and it irritated me that I seemed to be in so much demand until I saw the caller display and my heart beat a little faster.

"Beth, hi, I was just thinking about you. In fact, I've been thinking about you all day," I admitted, hoping it didn't sound too crass.

"Me too," she said, with a warmth in her voice that flushed away my doubts and uncertainties.

"Listen," she continued, "I don't have long but I wanted to tell you I called my policeman friend and, just as I thought, he'd be very interested in talking to you."

"Great."

"His name's Bruno Cannard and he's a Detective Inspector. Shall I give him your number?"

I felt my stomach lurch at the mention of his name.

"Martin? You've gone very quiet, are you alright?"

"Sorry, Beth. I'm fine, it's just that I already know him. He was the one who interviewed me about my assault. I'm afraid I wasn't as helpful as I might've been and I don't think he likes me much as a result."

"He's a good man, Martin, and he's been chasing after Leon for years now. Believe me, if he thinks he can get to him through you, you'll be his new best friend!"

I sighed. "OK, I've got his number; I'll give him a call. Thanks Beth."

"You're welcome."

There was an awkward pause and then she said, "I'd better be going, the place is heaving."

I swallowed, knowing it was now or maybe never. "Can I see you again, Beth?"

Without any noticeable hesitation she said, "Yes, that would be lovely."

"I'm working tonight, for you know who..."

"And I can't do tomorrow night."

I felt relieved to hear that because I didn't want to stand up Ella two nights in a row.

"The day after?" I asked.

"Great," she said.

"I'll take you out for a meal if you like – which do you prefer Italian, Chinese, Indian, or traditional English?"

"I like them all – surprise me."

CHAPTER TWENTY-SEVEN

That evening I climbed into the van with some trepidation, wondering what the night would bring. I hoped whatever it was that it didn't entail driving to Birmingham or some other place miles away. I was tired and smiled once again as I thought back to the cause of my tiredness.

I picked up Winsome at the prearranged spot at precisely seven thirty and was quite surprised to find him waiting alone.

"Where's Mike?" I asked.

"He'll be joining us shortly," Winsome growled. "We need to go to City Road."

"Is that the final destination, or just where we're picking up Mike?"

"What's this, the effing Spanish inquisition?"

"I just wondered how far we're going tonight."

"D'you fill the tank up like I tell you every time we go out on a job?"

"Yes, of course I did."

"Well, what's the problem?"

"Just curious, that's all. And wondering how long we'll be."

"Why, you gotta a hot date for later or something?"

I swallowed; did they know about me and Beth already? Were they watching me all the time? "No," I gave a strangled laugh, "I should be so lucky!"

"It'll take as long as it takes," Winsome said in a tone that suggested the conversation was over.

But I wasn't having it tonight. "Why does it always have to be like this?" I asked.

Winsome gave an exasperated sigh. "Like what?"

"Like I'm just a gofer who can't be trusted with any information."

"We've had this conversation before. I told you, the less you know the less information you can give the police if it all goes tits up."

"So you think I can't be trusted not to blab to the cops?"

Winsome sighed again. "Look, Marty, it's not like that at all; it's for yer own good."

I wasn't going to quit. "Why can't I be the judge of what's good for me – I am a grown man you know!"

"OK – I'll tell you the reason why we don't give you much notice. It's not that we don't trust you about grassing up, even you ain't that stupid – it's yer commitment that we sometimes doubt. Every time we do a job you wear a face like a smacked arse with disapproval oozing out of you like a Mother Superior. We need a van driver for this work and you accepted the work but we fear if we give too much away you'd chicken out and not turn up. Fact is Marty, you took this job knowing what Leon told you about it and you take his money and so in that respect you're no fucking different to the rest of us!"

I felt shocked by the venom in Winsome's voice. I hadn't expected this outburst and wondered how I should respond. How honest could I be with this man? I decided to stick as closely to the truth as I dared.

"I suppose you're right," I said. "Sometimes this line of work is way outside my comfort zone. You've got to remember I've been a banker most of my life where honesty and reputation counted for everything. So I won't deny it, operating outside of the law does present me with some personal challenges. But I do understand I'm being paid to do a job and it's true that Leon did warn me about the nature of some of his work. And I've always done what's been asked of me and kept my mouth shut, even though some of it goes against everything I've valued in the past. So I'm sorry if I don't always do it with a smile on my face."

Winsome eyed me sideways, looking thoughtful. "Well said, young Marty, thanks for being so honest with me. I'm still not gonna tell you what we're up to tonight because I can tell you now you ain't gonna like it but if you come through this job OK then we'll think about including you more in future. Leon has specifically requested yer presence on this one and I can't say no more."

"You've got me really worried now!" I said, feeling the familiar cramps in my bowels.

"Just drive and do exactly what I tell you and you'll be OK."

I tried to ease my grip on the steering wheel and relax my body. I really didn't want to ask Winsome if I could stop the van to use the loo. The pains subsided and, for the moment at least, I felt some measure of control.

We were getting close to City Road now and Winsome sat forward attentively. A parking space lay just ahead and he told me to pull in and wait.

"So what now?" I asked. I went to turn off the engine.

"Leave it running," Winsome said. "We wait for two rings on my phone from Mike – remember to do exactly what I say. We're gonna have to move fast shortly and we can't afford to screw up as we won't get another chance to do what needs to be done, so stay focused, Marty. Got that?"

I nodded and looked at the mobile phone Winsome was turning over and over in his hands. Adrenalin pumped through my body now as I wondered just what the hell was going down.

I didn't have to wait long. The phone trilled twice and then fell silent. We'd both seen Mike's name on caller display so knew it was the signal we'd been waiting for.

Winsome turned to me and said, "Pull out and take the first turning left. You should see Mike walking a few yards behind another guy. I want you to pull up just in front of the other guy. Got it?"

I nodded. "What then?" I asked.

"There may be a bit of rough stuff so you stay in the van and wait until I get back in – then we make a delivery."

There was no time for more questions because I'd already spotted Mike's huge frame following another guy down the street. I drove as instructed and stopped a few feet ahead of the guy. This seemed to spook him because he immediately looked over his shoulder, saw Mike bearing down on him and turned to run. By then Winsome had already jumped out of the passenger door and blocked his path. The man tried to run into the road but the side of the van effectively blocked his path. He threw a punch which Winsome easily side-stepped. As he tried to throw another, Winsome landed an uppercut under the man's chin that sent his head snapping back. Mike was waiting behind him and coshed him over the head. The fight was over and had lasted no more than a few seconds. The rear doors opened and I stared in disbelief as Mike and Winsome manhandled the unconscious man into the van. Mike climbed in the back with him and then I heard the doors closing and saw Winsome scurrying towards the passenger door with his awkward lolling gait.

"OK, drive," he said, breathlessly.

I accelerated away and asked, "Where to?"

Winsome gave directions, his breathing laboured.

He'd been right – I wasn't happy to be involved in what looked like a kidnapping – another crime to add to what was becoming a long list. Bearing in mind our earlier conversation, I made a conscious effort not to allow my concerns to show on my face but I'm not sure how well I succeeded.

"Who's the passenger?" I asked, with a throat that felt dry and constricted.

"Someone who owes Leon a lot of money," Winsome replied.

"What's going to happen to him?"

"Depends how soon he can pay."

"Times are hard," I observed dryly. "What if he can't pay?"

Winsome looked at me. "Then tomorrow night we may have to visit another of Leon's landscape gardening clients," he said, grimly.

I pulled into an industrial estate on the outskirts of Rumney and Winsome told me to stop outside an unmarked warehouse. He took a small wireless transmitting key fob from his pocket and pressed a button. A few seconds later a large rollover garage door began to slide open and I drove straight into a large cavernous space. A light must have been triggered by a movement detector. Winsome pressed another button and the doors began to close behind us. Once we were safely shut in, he got out of the van and went around to open the rear doors.

Mike emerged with a grin pulling the comatose man along the floor behind him. Winsome said to me, "Give Mike a hand to get him out."

He took his phone out and pressed a speed dial button. He waited only long enough for the phone to ring twice then cut off the call. I guessed it was another signal to someone.

The man looked to be in his mid-thirties with dark hair and a sallow complexion. His wrists were bound with strong black gaffer tape and a short strip had also been placed over his mouth. He was thin but surprisingly heavy to lift from the van.

We took an arm each and dragged his body across the

floor until Mike said, "This will do. Keep him upright for me."

He let go of the man's arm and I supported his weight as best I could while he took a large remote control box from the wall. This turned out to be the operating console for some lifting gear that ran along the ceiling of the warehouse on high tracks. Mike expertly manoeuvred the gear until the large hook was directly above the man and then lowered it until it came to rest just above his head. He placed the man's tied wrists on the hook and raised him up like a sack of potatoes. Apparently satisfied, he left him dangling about a foot off the ground then said to me, "Help me take off his clothes."

As Mike began unbuckling the guy's belt, I removed his expensive-looking shoes and then yanked off his trousers folding them and placing them carefully on the shoes. The clothes were good quality. Mike unbuttoned the man's leather jacket and then took a large pair of scissors and proceeded to ruin the jacket by cutting off the sleeves. The shirt suffered the same fate. Now the man was naked but for a pair of Calvin Klein boxer shorts. "Don't be shy," Mike said, pulling the pants off and tossing them onto the top of the pile of clothes.

The man hadn't stirred through any of this and now dangled on the hook like a carcass in a butcher shop. His head rested on his chin as he spun slowly around and around.

Then Leon arrived carrying a wooden baseball bat in his right hand. He had a crazed look on his face that made me wonder if he had been taking drugs, but then I realised that it was anticipation of violence to come that was making him high. He nodded at all those present, clearly enjoying having an audience.

"Wake him up!" he commanded.

Mike obliged by throwing a bucket of cold water over the man who woke up instantly looking around himself in obvious panic. He bucked and strained, kicking the air like a condemned man who had just been dropped with a noose around his neck. His eyes were wide with fear and strange whimpering noises escaped from his mouth as the gaffer tape prevented him from speaking.

I watched in silence, fearing for the man and for myself as I wondered what horrors I was about to witness. Eventually the man stopped his futile struggles and became still. He slowly span around on the rope but turned his head so that his eyes never left Leon's face except for a moment at the full extent of the spin. Leon took the remote console and raised him until his naked feet were suspended at waist height to the rest of us. Then he stared malevolently at him, smacking the baseball bat into the palm of his hand.

"You owe me money!" he said.

The man looked imploringly at him, trying hard to speak but all that came out were muffled grunts.

"Don't waste your time trying to speak to me," Leon said. "The time for excuses is long past. You've had plenty of chances and all I've heard is one excuse after another."

As the man spun slowly around Leon suddenly lunged at him with the baseball bat catching him squarely on the fleshy part of the buttocks. There was a loud slap as the bat made contact and the blow sent the man's skinny body into the air making him swing violently back and forth. His legs kicked and his eyes watered. I saw a red weal on his backside in the shape of the bat.

Leon laughed at his discomfort. He waited until the man stopped bucking and swinging on the rope.

"So why didn't you pay me what you owed when you had the chance?"

The man made pathetic mewing sounds as he tried to answer.

Leon nodded in mock sympathy and said, "I've told you once already it's too late for excuses!" Then he smacked him hard again on the other buttock. Once again the man writhed in pain and began spinning around.

I couldn't help clenching my own buttocks at the thought of the man's pain and discomfort. I could feel the bile rising in my throat and swallowed hard. I felt nauseous and wondered how much more of the violence I could take before throwing up.

Leon was clearly enjoying himself. When the man eventually stopped spinning around and became still once more, Leon asked, "Do you know you have twenty-six bones in each foot?"

The man just hung forlornly in front of him, making no attempt to answer.

"That's fifty-two in both feet, nearly a quarter of all the bones in the human body."

Leon stared at the man, leaving him to contemplate what was coming next.

I felt my fingernails digging into my palms as I sensed the man's fear.

"Have you ever wondered how many of those bones I could break with one good blow from this baseball bat? Let's see, shall we?"

He held the bat so that it hovered just above the man's foot like he was taking careful aim at the most bony part. The man remained still, apparently frozen in terror. Leon took a big swing and just as the bat arced down the man moved his foot and Leon missed. The momentum of the swing took the bat into the air causing Leon to stumble and nearly lose his balance.

"God dammit!" he cried. "How dare you move your foot! You won't do that again, you bastard! Mike, hold his leg still for me."

Mike immediately took one of the man's legs and held it firmly at the knee. Leon took aim again with the bat. The man tried to wriggle but Mike had a firm grip on his knee and the foot remained perfectly still.

Leon then swung the bat high into the air and brought it down hard. There was a sickening crunch of flesh and bone as this time the bat found its target. Even through the gaffer tape the man's scream of pain was evident.

This was too much for me. I turned away and vomited.

Leon laughed. "Look at the mess you've made now," he mocked. "You're going to have to toughen up working for me, Martin – come here and hold his other leg so I can see if we can't break a few more bones this time."

I shook my head. "C-can't," I stuttered.

"Oh yes you bloody well can!" he declared, putting his face right in front of mine. "Unless you fancy being the next one to hang from the ceiling for some sport."

He shoved me towards the man who looked to be in agony, his face screwed tightly as tears squeezed from his eyes.

Knowing I had no choice. I took hold of the other leg tucking my elbows into my ribs to stop my hands shaking. My eyes never left the man's foot as Leon drew a careful bead on it. At the moment of impact I shut my eyes but I could still hear the sickening thwack as the bat struck the foot and feel the man's tremors of pain through my hands. I let go and stepped away, unable to look up at the man's face anymore. I felt ashamed at my complete inability to stand up to Leon.

The man hung limply now.

"Wake him up again," Leon demanded.

Mike threw another bucket of water over the man who stirred slowly back into consciousness.

Leon tossed the bat onto the floor and then took up a pair of bolt cutters that had been leaning against a wall. He held the points near the man's groin and said, "Shall we cut his cock off next?"

I held my breath, too terrified to move or make any protest.

The man's eyes widened in horror and Leon laughed out loud.

"Hold his hand out, Mike," he commanded.

Mike obeyed and, in one quick motion, Leon snipped the man's little finger off and deftly caught the bloody stump as it fell away. The man bucked and reared once more whining like a dog.

"Now here's what we're going to do," he said, looking up triumphantly at his victim. "We're going to send your finger to your lovely wife and tell her that if she ever wants to see the rest of you again she'll have to find all the money you owe by five o'clock tomorrow. Otherwise that's all she'll ever have of you to bury."

He dropped the bolt cutters on the warehouse floor and tossed the finger to Winsome who caught it and quickly wrapped it in a tissue paper.

Leon turned to me and nodding towards the discarded torture instruments said, "Lose those in a place where no one will ever find them."

Then he turned abruptly on his heels and marched out the door. My hands shook as I bent down to pick up the bloodied bolt cutter and baseball bat. I thought my legs might buckle underneath me. I felt relieved that no one appeared to be taking any notice of me. I hoped and prayed that they wouldn't ask me to deliver the finger to the poor bloke's wife! I looked at the poor soul hanging there the floor beneath him was patterned with spots of his own blood as he swung to and fro.

"What's going to happen to him?" I asked Winsome.

"Depends whether or not his missus comes up with the readies by the deadline. Until then he's just gonna have to hang around here." He laughed at his own sick joke.

"Do you need me any more tonight?"

"Na, you can bugger off – make sure you get rid of that stuff you're carrying soon as – and remember, it mustn't be found!"

"Yeah, I got that message loud and clear, thanks."

I dropped the items in the back of the van. They had Leon's fingerprints on them and the victim's blood. I'd already made up my mind I was going to take them to DI Bruno Cannard. Surely this would be enough to convict Leon and send him down for a long time. I couldn't stand by and let a man die if there was a chance of saving him. It was eleven-thirty, as soon as I got back to the relative safety of the flat I pulled out Cannard's card from my wallet and dialled his mobile number.

It went straight to voicemail. Bloody unbelievable!

I left a message for him to call me back urgently but knew it wasn't enough. I had to do something more. To hell with the consequences – I took out the supposedly untraceable mobile phone from Cooper's Logistics and dialled 999.

CHAPTER TWENTY-EIGHT

I paced up and down my small flat – couldn't think of sleep. If I did doze I'd only end up having nightmares about the beating I'd just witnessed. An hour passed and nothing happened except my frustrations grew and grew. Then finally at 1:30am my phone rang. It was DI Cannard.

He apologised for the lateness of the hour but reminded me I did say it was urgent. His voice sounded weary.

"I need to talk to you about Leon Cooper," I said.

"Can it wait until morning?"

"Beth said you're a decent guy and that I could trust you. Some of what I say may need to be off the record."

There was a silence at the end of the phone and I was beginning to wonder if he was still there when he said, "OK, I'm listening."

"We need a long chat and I'd prefer to do it face-to-face, but before that there's something urgent I need to tell you."

I explained recent events and the anonymous 999 call I'd made.

When I'd finished he said, "I need to find out what the response was. Give me five minutes and I'll call you back."

He took ten minutes to call back.

"They sent a car in immediate response to your call but when the officers arrived at the warehouse the place was deserted, no lights, no vehicles and no sounds coming from inside."

"Did they go inside?" I asked.

"The doors were locked; they shone a torch through a window but saw nothing suspicious that could justify them breaking in without a warrant."

"But the bloke could've been left hanging there unconscious!" I said, incredulously.

"I doubt Cooper would have left him there unguarded. They will have moved him somewhere else and if we go charging in and show our hand he'll know something's up. Tell me, does Cooper trust you?"

I thought about that. "I think on some level he does but he doesn't share his plans with me and I often feel like I'm being tested."

"That sounds about right. Can you come into the station tomorrow morning?"

"I'd rather meet somewhere more anonymous. Every time I've come in the past he seems to know about it – he may have someone inside tipping him off."

This was greeted with more silence at the other end of the line. Eventually Cannard said, "In that case do you know the pub called The Woodcutter?"

I knew it – it was an upmarket place towards Caerphilly. We agreed to meet there at 11 o'clock.

Cannard's parting shot was, "Make sure no one is following you."

I hadn't considered that Leon might be having me followed and the thought unnerved me even more. I twitched the curtains, half expecting to see some shadowy figure leaning on a lamp post. As far as I could tell the street was empty. I set my alarm but it was quite unnecessary – I lay on the bed but sleep simply wouldn't come.

*

Next morning, I walked into town and popped into Beth's Café for a coffee and a breakfast roll, and had a whispered conversation with Beth bringing her up to speed.

As usual she was very positive. "You're doing the right thing," she said. "Bruno Cannard is a good guy and he'll understand and appreciate that you won't want to do anything to place you or your family in peril."

I felt reassured, in fact I was pleased to be doing something at last. Outside the cafe I rang Patrick and told him what was happening too. He was equally encouraging, especially when he heard that I'd finally secured some hard evidence linking Leon directly to what was at the very least a serious assault.

"Go carefully, my friend," he said, "and let me know how it goes."

I wondered whether or not to drive the van to the pub or take a taxi. I didn't want to risk being followed and so decided on a taxi.

When the taxi dropped me at the pub, one glance at the BMWs and Mercedes in the car park told me this was a place where well off businessmen met to do deals over lunch. There were far more people in the pub than I'd anticipated but as soon as I walked in I spotted DI Cannard at the bar and walked over to him, scarcely glancing at the other punters. Cannard bought me a pint and we found a quiet alcove which perfectly suited our clandestine meeting.

"So what've you got for me?" Cannard asked, straight to the point as always.

I hesitated still a little unsure how much I should admit to and where exactly I should start.

"I want to help you put Leon Cooper behind bars. If possible I want to remain anonymous but if that's not possible, I want me and my family to go into a witness protection scheme. Oh, and I want complete immunity from any crimes I may implicate myself in."

"Bloody hell, you don't want much do you? Would you like a million pounds spending money in your new life too?" Cannard glared at me. "You've been watching too many films mate, we don't operate like that."

"Well what protection can you offer me? I'm putting my life on the line here, as I suspect you well know."

"A lot depends on what you can give us and whether or not it results in a conviction. Also, it depends what part you played in his criminal activities. If you've committed a serious crime yourself I can't guarantee you'd walk away scot-free but we could recommend leniency to the judge."

"What about protection for my family?"

"If we believe they're in danger we will do all we can to ensure their safety."

I weighed up what Cannard said. Beth said he was a trustworthy and good man but he didn't seem to be bending over backwards to offer his help. Maybe it was a negotiating ploy, or maybe he regarded me as a criminal. I could hardly blame him if he did. I wished now I'd asked Beth to put a good word in for me before approaching him but none of us had anticipated things happening so quickly. Then an idea occurred to me and I took out my mobile and rang Beth, praying she would pick up.

I was so relieved to hear her voice. "Hi Beth, if I pass the phone over to Inspector Cannard will you vouch for me and tell him I'm not a crook?"

I handed the phone to Cannard and the two of them chatted like such good friends that I had to suppress a pang of jealousy. I couldn't hear what Beth was saying but occasionally Cannard's assessing eyes lifted to me as if seeing me in a new light. After a short while he ended the call and handed my phone back.

"Beth speaks very highly of you, says you're an honest guy who's just got caught up in something and you're now in way over your head," Cannard said. "Is that true?"

I nodded.

"It had better be," he warned. "If I catch you messing

Beth around or ever letting her down you'll have far worse than the likes of Leon Copper to answer to!"

"I promise it's true. I had no idea what I was getting into," I said. "All I want is to extricate myself without me or my friends and family getting hurt. And if in doing that I help put a vicious thug like Cooper behind bars then so much the better."

"OK," Cannard said, "let's start from the beginning and you can tell me what you've been up to but don't you dare leave anything out."

I told him all about the shady late-night deals and the lengths we went to to avoid surveillance. I soon reached the part about the disposal of the body and hesitated wondering if I might incriminate myself. I took a deep breath and decided to continue, hoping I wouldn't live to regret the faith I was putting in Beth's judgement of this man.

Cannard held up his hand when he heard about the midnight landscaping escapade and said, "At this point, if I were playing by the book, I should arrest and caution you. By not doing so I want you to know I am going out on a limb for you, and for Beth. Please carry on."

I continued. When I reached the bit about disposing of the murder weapon, Cannard interrupted me again.

"How did you dispose of it?"

"He wanted me to drive far away and toss it into a river, but when it came to it, I decided to place it somewhere where it would not be easily discovered but where I could retrieve it if necessary."

"Good man!" Cannard said, clapping me on the back.

"I don't know that it was Leon who pulled the trigger on that occasion," I explained.

"All the same, if we have the body and the murder weapon there's a good chance forensics will find something on whoever did do it."

Moving on, I described the kidnapping and torture of the man last night. When I told of the baseball bat and the bolt cutters, Cannard's eyes flashed. "Do you still have these items?"

"They're in the back of my van."

"You've got them with you now?!"

"No, I came by taxi."

Cannard looked thoughtful. "We know now the warehouse is empty, so they must have moved him but there may still be forensic evidence which I think justifies a search of the place. Do you have a key?"

I shook my head.

Cannard frowned. "It would've been good to catch Leon and his cohorts on the premises red-handed. We need to find this guy before they kill him. At least we have the torture weapons and you said Leon was definitely not wearing gloves or anything; is that correct?"

I recalled the horrible scenes from last night and said, "No he was definitely holding the bat and the bolt-cutters in his bare hands."

"That was careless of him. I need to make some calls," Cannard said, pulling his Blackberry out of his pocket.

While he spoke urgently to his colleagues, I stared absent-mindedly at the bar only half listening to what was being said. I realised that now I'd made this move and involved the police there was no turning back. Some kind of sixth sense made me aware that someone was watching me in the mirror behind the bar and suddenly I felt a cold chill run down my spine. Leon Cooper was looking straight at me. Our eyes met briefly before Leon broke the contact and turned away calmly carrying his drinks to a table off to our left. My pulse was racing. I was certain Leon had spotted me and that he would have seen Cannard sitting next to me. I was equally sure that my face will have registered shock, fright and guilt in the few short seconds that Leon had been watching me. Damn! My cover was blown already! What the hell was I supposed to do now?

CHAPTER TWENTY-NINE

Fighting down the urge to run, I checked the other mirrors to make sure Leon wasn't watching from any other angle and then, satisfied there was no line of sight, I waved frantically to get Cannard's attention.

Into the phone, Cannard said, "Hold on a moment," and then to me, "What is it?"

"Leon's here, in the pub!" I struggled to keep my voice low.

The colour drained from Cannard's face as he looked around. "Where?"

"In an alcove around there," I said, pointing in the direction Leon had gone.

"Did he see you?"

"Yes, I'm certain he did, we made eye contact."

"Shit!"

Cannard spoke into the phone. "Something's come up, I'll call you back."

He ended the call and said, "Where's Leon now?"

"I told you, just to our left, in an alcove so we can't see him from here but we'll have to pass by to get out!" I could hear my voice rising.

"Ok, here's what we'll do. It's better if Leon thinks

we're still here having another drink. I know the guy behind the bar and so I'm going to go and buy us some more drinks in full view of Leon and bring them back to the table here. Then we'll leave the drinks and the owner will let us out of the back door. I'm pretty certain Leon won't be able to see us sneaking out in any mirrors so it should buy us a little time to get a head start on him."

I felt doubtful. "What if he was here when we arrived? He may have seen us coming in and not just now when I went to the bar."

"Well that's a chance we'll just have to take."

Cannard put his plan into action, first going to the bar to buy two drinks and then carrying them back to our table without appearing to give a sideways glance in Leon's direction.

"He's still there having a drink and a laugh with his cronies. Looks like they're in for a session, so with a bit of luck we'll have a clear run."

I followed him to the rear door where the barman stood waiting with a key in his hand. Cannard led me to his unmarked Saab and told me to keep my head down until they were out of the car park just to be on the safe side.

Once we were on the road I sat up and said, "What now?"

"We need to get to that warehouse and take a look inside."

I was going to say I didn't think it was a good idea but thought better of it – where the hell else was I going to go. At least with solid detective by my side I felt relatively safe.

The warehouse looked deserted when we arrived – it was the perfect location to keep someone against their will because it was isolated in its own private compound with a high chain-link fence all around it. There were no vehicles anywhere in sight and the gate at the entrance was padlocked. I'd half expected the place to be surrounded with police officers.

"They're on their way," Cannard said, as if reading my

mind. He was busy picking the padlock with some kind of tool he'd extracted from his pocket. "Let's see if we can get in shall we?"

"Shouldn't we wait until the others get here?" I asked, looking over my shoulder.

"Na, we'll be OK. It doesn't look like there's anyone about and even if they are inside, the cavalry are only five minutes away tops." He smiled triumphantly and threw open the gates, dropping the padlock onto the ground.

Cannard parked his car around the side of the warehouse, out of sight of the road, and we walked around to the entrance. Cannard studied the lock and said, "This shouldn't give us too much trouble." He fished out his lock picks again and after just a second or two flung the doors wide. I couldn't help thinking he should have had a warrant or something but felt I'd already asked enough stupid questions.

The inside of the warehouse was as gloomy and cavernous just as I remembered it. We stood listening for a few seconds before entering but there was no sound from within. Cannard found the light switch and suddenly the whole place was bathed in harsh fluorescent light.

To my utter dismay, the place had been scrubbed completely clean...

The ceiling hook from which the man had been suspended was gleaming and clean and reflected the light right back at us. The concrete floor that had been pooled with blood was bleached clean and a strong smell of disinfectant lingered in the air.

Cannard looked disappointed. "You're sure this is the right warehouse?" he asked.

"Of course I am," I snapped, "I was only here last night."

"Then Leon must have ordered his men to move very fast to scrub the place down and remove all evidence. Forensics may get lucky but I doubt it."

I blinked in disbelief. How could it be possible for

Leon to move so fast? I looked again at the hoist where, less than twelve hours ago, a man had been left dangling with two broken feet. I looked at the floor where the blood from his severed finger had pooled. All that was there now was a uniformly cleaned stretch of bare concrete. For a second, I even wondered if Cannard was right and I'd inadvertently brought him to the wrong warehouse but no, I was absolutely certain this was the place.

Cannard sighed and said, "Well there's no point in us hanging around here. Let's go to your van and pick up the weapons used in this alleged torture."

His casual use of the word 'alleged' annoyed me. "I can assure there's nothing '*alleged*' about it. I was here, in this very place last night and witnessed Leon savagely beating a man who was left dangling from that hook. You have to believe me!"

"I want to believe you, Martin, but without any evidence to put before a judge we have nothing and so it remains 'alleged' until you can prove otherwise."

"Come on," I said. "The evidence is in my van."

We drove across Cardiff to my flat in silence and Cannard pulled up his car facing opposite my van. My heart sank as I noticed a splattering of broken glass on the pavement close to the driver's door. I jumped out of the car and cursed when I saw the gaping hole where the window had been. Cannard joined me on the pavement, saying nothing as he surveyed the scene of the break in.

"This is the second time my van's been broken into since I've been living here," I said.

"Whole area's a bit of a black spot for this kind of thing, mostly juveniles to blame. We catch the little buggers but there's not much we can do and within hours they're back on the streets doing it all over again."

I went around the back of the van and tried the doors. As expected they'd already been unlocked. The bolt cutters and the blood-stained baseball bat with Leon's fingerprints on them were gone and there was a strong smell of disinfectant similar to that in the warehouse.

"They're gone," I said, making no attempt to keep the despair from my voice.

We stood looking into the cavernous space inside the empty van. Cannard ran his fingers across the metal floor. "Still damp," he said, looking around him as if expecting witnesses to materialise. Sadly this was not the kind of area where curtains twitched at every noise in the street and even if any of the local residents had seen anything they knew better than to get involved with the police. "They can't have been here very long ago. Let's go and check your flat."

I hadn't considered that they may have broken into my flat as well. I went up to the front door which, as usual, had been left on the latch by one of the other residents despite the landlord's instructions to the contrary. My flat was on the first floor and I took the stairs two at a time with Cannard close on my heels. The door to my flat was locked, much as I'd left it this morning, but I remembered Winsome's warning about how easy it was to get in. I hadn't had time to do anything about the locks. I fished in my pocket for the keys.

It was immediately evident before either of us crossed the threshold that the flat had been ransacked and trashed.

"Oh shit! What have we unleashed?" I asked, looking at my possessions scattered all over the floor. Every room was the same; drawers had been pulled out and tipped upside down to spread their contents over the floor. Cupboards had been emptied and the contents similarly strewn about the place. Anything glass had been smashed, including my television. The few pictures I'd hung had been torn down and smashed onto the floor. The bedding had been stripped off my bed and thrown on the floor, and the mattress slashed open. In the sitting room the armchairs had all also been slashed and their stuffing was bulging through the slits.

Just the one armchair remained intact and I dropped into it but quickly jumped out again. The cushion felt wet and I brought my fingers up to my nose. "The bastards have even pissed on my chair!" I cried.

"Well, at least we'll have their DNA," Cannard observed wryly. "Have you got somewhere you can stay the night?"

1 thought immediately of Patrick and nodded.

"Well I suggest you go there and lay low for a bit. It may not be safe for you to hang around here as Leon may come looking for you. I need to go back to the station and start things rolling. We'll send the scenes of crime officers around here straight from the warehouse. Meanwhile, you have a think of anything else you can give us on Leon's activities and I'll need you to give a statement in the morning. OK?"

"Yes. I'm sorry the evidence I had was snatched."

"Not your fault," Cannard reassured, but his eyes reflected my own disappointment. "I'll give you a call in the morning when it's a good time for you to come in. Meanwhile try not to worry; we'll nail this bastard somehow or another. Can I drop you anywhere?"

"It's OK. I'll take the van and get the window fixed."

"Can't do that I'm afraid, forensics will have to go over it before I can release it to you."

"In that case you can drop me in town, please? I need to check my friend's willing to put me up for the night."

I felt pretty sure Patrick would be fine about me staying, but I wasn't about to share my plans for the remainder of the afternoon with Cannard. There was one other piece of evidence that I felt sure Leon couldn't know about that I could still retrieve. As soon as Cannard drove off I backtracked to a car hire firm to hire something nice and anonymous.

CHAPTER THIRTY

I drove the hire car fast and hard, wanting to get to the Welsh Borders and back in time to meet Ella as promised later that evening. It seemed a long way and my mind was racing faster than the car. I was amazed by how fast Leon had moved to eradicate the evidence and break into my van and flat, because I was certain it was on his orders. One thing was certain, the game was up for me where Leon was concerned – not that I cared, but I was worried what Leon might do to me if he managed to catch me. Even though I was in an anonymous hire car, I was feeling paranoid enough to check my mirrors every few miles to be sure no one was following me.

Finally, I found the lay-by near the picnic area where I'd first thought to throw the gun into the river. This was one piece of incriminating evidence that Leon couldn't get to first.

I'd been fairly certain I would remember the place it was buried, but now I was here the foliage had changed and the shrubbery had grown much thicker. I scratched my head and looked around trying desperately to remember the exact spot. Panic gripped me until I finally recognised a tree and located the right place.

I scrabbled around in the dirt beneath a large bramble bush and sure enough, the orange supermarket bag that I'd wrapped the gun in broke the surface. Carefully, I removed the oily rag I'd wrapped around the gun and it appeared to have kept it in pristine condition. I only handled it by the barrel so that in the unlikely event of there being fingerprints I wouldn't smudge them. Actually, when I thought about it, I remembered handling the gun when I buried it so my own prints were definitely on it. I wondered if handing it in to the police I may end up putting myself in the frame as the murderer. Dare I take that chance? What choices did I have?

I returned to the car and placed the gun under the driver's seat. I'd have plenty of time to think about what to do on the long drive back. I checked my watch; with a bit of luck, if the traffic wasn't too heavy, I'd still make it back in time to meet Ella at the restaurant. What if Leon threatened Ella? I'd planned to warn her when we got together but now wondered if I should stop the car and call her mobile. Better to be safe than sorry. Maybe I should warn Katrina too, but then Leon would hardly threaten her now we'd separated. I was pretty sure Leon knew nothing about my blossoming relationship with Beth so she should be safe. I also decided to ring Patrick just to warn him that things had moved on considerably since we last spoke. I tried Ella's mobile first but couldn't get through; she'd ring me back when she saw the missed call. Patrick was unavailable too; probably with a client or, more likely given that it was coming up to four thirty, he'd switched it off when he was with a client and forgotten to switch it back on. I left him a warning message and said I'd explain more when I saw him.

The gun under my seat made me feel very self-conscious. I was keen to pass it over to Cannard as soon as possible so that it was out of my possession. I glanced at my watch. I'd already lost too much time as I didn't want to be late for Ella. Cannard would insist that I deliver it straight away. He certainly wouldn't want it to fall back into Leon's hands like the bolt cutters and the baseball bat.

In the end I decided to leave the gun under the driver's seat. After all, unlike the van – there was nothing to associate the hire car with me other than the hire firm's records and I doubted Leon's reach stretched that far.

I'd have liked to nip home and have a shower before meeting Ella but knew they would almost certainly be watching the flat. I wondered if Leon would be watching Patrick's place too. He knew we were friends. I decided it wasn't fair to put him at risk. I pulled over and tried his mobile again but still got put straight through to voicemail. I tried Ella again but she still didn't answer.

I tried Beth and she picked up straight away.

"Hi Beth," I said, relieved to hear her voice. "Listen, things are kicking off with Leon and it's not safe for me to go to my flat right now. I'm meeting Ella at seven o'clock so is it OK if I drop by your place and have a quick shower? I'm sorry to be so cheeky!"

"Of course it's OK," she said, "and after seeing Ella you can come back here and stay the night if you want."

"That's really kind of you Beth. Just so you know, I'm in a hire car and not the van – it's a silver hatchback." I realised I didn't even know the make of car. I glanced at the badge in the centre of the steering wheel. "A Vauxhall."

"What's going on with Leon?" Beth asked, a note of concern creeping into her voice.

"It's a long story. I'll tell you when I see you."

*

By the time I turned into Beth's drive I'd already decided not to mention the gun under the car seat. I had considered giving it to Beth for safe keeping but didn't want to compromise her, or worse, place her in any kind of danger. She opened the front door before I got to it and ushered me in, looking over my shoulder to check no one was watching.

I told her everything that had happened earlier that day but left out the part about retrieving the gun that afternoon. The fewer people who knew about that it the better.

Beth was naturally concerned and fully understood why I couldn't go back to the flat. "You must stay here tonight," she insisted.

"I don't want you to be in any danger," I insisted. "Besides, Patrick has agreed I can stay with him until all this blows over."

"But Leon knows you're friends with Patrick, and that would be the first place he'll look. Whereas I'm pretty sure he doesn't know about us — so you'd be much safer here. I'm not taking no for an answer, Martin. You're staying here and that's that!"

Beth could be formidable when she wanted to be and I had no further choice in the matter. I felt absurdly grateful to her and gave her a big hug, which turned into a deep, lasting kiss.

We broke apart breathlessly and, in a husky voice, Beth said, "Not now. You go and have that shower and meet your daughter — I'll wait up for you..."

Half an hour later my step was decidedly lighter when I approached the Indian restaurant to meet Ella. We'd agreed to meet just inside in the small bar area. I ordered a glass of wine and wondered if I should order a diet cola for Ella or wait and see what she wanted. I decided it would be better to wait — she was changing so fast now she was at uni that her tastes may well have changed too.

The door opened behind me and I turned expectantly but it was another couple arriving for a meal. I took my glass of wine and chose a seat facing the door so I could watch out for her.

Fifteen minutes passed and several more customers arrived but there was no sign of Ella. She was always a few minutes late so I wasn't unduly worried. After half an hour my wine glass was empty and I kept glancing at my watch. I kept checking my phone for a message.

I checked my watch again. It wasn't like Ella to be this late and not text or call. Perhaps she was having trouble getting a signal, or she'd let her battery get too low. A waiter came to take away my empty glass and ask if I wanted another.

"No thanks," I replied. "I'll wait for my daughter to arrive – she'll be here any minute."

The waiter gave a slight smile that didn't reach his eyes and went back to the bar.

I took my phone out again, turning it over and over in my hands wondering if I should call her but not wanting our evening together to get off to a bad start with her accusing me of nagging.

Then the phone suddenly bleeped making me almost drop it in surprise. The caller display showed Ella's number and I felt a mixture of annoyance that she'd left it so long to get in touch and relief that she had finally thought to do so. She seemed to be sending me a picture message. The signal in the restaurant was weak and it was taking an age to download. I watched the little swirling circle of dots as the photo slowly revealed itself starting at the top of the screen and working down.

I couldn't make out what it was and reached in my pocket for my reading glasses. The top quarter of the screen had downloaded now and what I saw turned my blood cold. A pair of bound slender wrists were hanging from a hook. I didn't recognise the wrists but I knew exactly where the hook was located. Frustratingly slowly the picture revealed itself. I could see elbows now and the top of a head crowned in luxuriant, red hair.

I fought my shaking hands to hold the phone as still as I could. The face slowly revealed itself and as the terrified eyes were revealed there could be no more room for doubt. The bastards had Ella in the warehouse dangling on a hook and as the photo finally finished downloading I saw she was naked.

The photo flipped over to reveal a chilling message that read *'If you're not here in thirty minutes I'll bite off her nipples. Any sign of police and she dies!'*

I could feel the heat rising in my cheeks as my heart started pounding blood. An involuntary gasp escaped my lips and the waiter, who had been hovering nearby said, "Is everything alright sir?"

"No, it bloody well isn't!" I snapped, then quickly realised it was hardly the waiter's fault. "I'm sorry," I quickly added, and thrust a twenty-pound note into his hand. "I have to go. This should cover the glass of wine and you can keep the change."

I'd already exited through the door before he could thank me.

When I reached the hire car I was sweating profusely, somehow I fumbled the key into the ignition. My initial instinct was to drive straight around there and use the gun under my seat to rescue Ella. But I'd never fired a gun and didn't even know if there were any bullets left in it. I glanced around to ensure there were no passers-by and took it out from under the seat, carefully unwrapping it. It weighed heavily in my hands as I examined it looking for a safety lock which I felt sure must be there somewhere: Didn't all guns have them these days? I found what I thought might be the safety catch and gingerly moved it, making sure the nozzle was pointing down and away from me, just in case. The magazine popped out of the handle into the palm of my hand. I dropped it but it fell harmlessly into my lap. There were five bullets inside so that at least answered the question was it loaded. I pushed the magazine back into the handle of the gun and watched the spring-loaded leaver click back into place.

There was another smaller lever just above the trigger on the left hand side of the gun that could be operated by the thumb when holding the grip. I decided this had to be the safety catch but there was nothing to indicate whether it was on or off. I didn't want to waste a shot just to find out but then I had the bright idea of ejecting the magazine again, catching it neatly this time instead of just letting it fall into my lap. Even though the magazine was in my hand, which suggested the gun was empty, for all I knew there may be a bullet in the breach, or barrel, or whatever it was called, so I still took great care to ensure the gun was pointing away from me as I cautiously attempted to squeeze the trigger. At first, nothing happened but I had no idea how much strength was needed so gradually applied more force through my trigger finger. Nothing, the trigger wouldn't budge. Surely that meant the safety switch must be on. I moved it with my thumb to the second position and began to gently squeeze the trigger again. This time I felt it move instantly in response to gentle pressure. That was another question answered. I didn't try to squeeze it all the way just in case it went off. If there was a bullet already inside the thing I didn't want to waste it, neither did I want to damage the hire car or attract any unwanted attention. I felt a little more confident that the gun would fire if I absolutely needed it to. I hoped and prayed that simply pointing it at Leon and threatening to shoot would be sufficient to make him release Ella.

CHAPTER THIRTY-ONE

The drive to the warehouse was about fifteen minutes. When I got to within five hundred yards of the place I pulled over because there was one more thing I had to do.

If I didn't manage to rescue Ella then we'd probably both be killed but, just in case we survived a little longer than expected, I forwarded the photo and its chilling message to DI Cannard. I added just one word in capitals – *'HELP!'*

I hoped and prayed that Cannard would have his phone switched on and that I could count on him to be discreet. I wanted to get there before any police did in case they were spotted by Leon, and Ella was harmed as a result.

I spotted two people sitting in a 4x4 on the approach road and guessed they were Leon's men keeping a watch. Their eyes followed my progress as I passed and I could see one of them talking into his phone. They made no attempt to follow me – they already knew where I was headed. As I parked the car just outside the warehouse doors my phone rang.

It was Cannard and his voice sounded urgent and commanding. "Martin, you must not attempt to go in there alone. Leave it to us, do you hear me?!"

"I hear you but it's too late; I'm right outside now. I'll leave the phone switched on so you can hear what's going on. Oh, and there are two men outside keeping watch in a black 4x4."

"I'm ordering you..." I took the phone from my ear and heard Cannard's protesting voice growing weaker as I turned down the volume. I slipped the phone down the front of my underpants hoping that the material wouldn't muffle the sound too much. Then I took the gun from underneath the seat and set the safety catch to what I thought was off, then I tucked it into my waistband and right at the centre of my back just as I'd seen Mike and Winsome do so many times before. Then I took a deep breath and went inside the warehouse.

Much to my surprise, it wasn't empty as it had been earlier. There were crates stacked floor to ceiling that effectively blocked my view and formed a narrow corridor within the warehouse.

Winsome was waiting just inside the door and said, "Sorry, Marty, I gotta frisk you."

I remained facing towards him and raised both arms up. Winsome tapped my sides and felt my pockets and then he ran his hands up the insides of my thighs. He missed the mobile phone and started to reach around to rub down my back.

"For crying out loud," I said. "Stop pissing about and take me to my daughter will you!"

My ruse worked! He looked distinctly embarrassed and I capitalised on this by adding, "You know I haven't got anything on me, I'm not that stupid."

"Sorry, mate, you know the drill," Winsome muttered, but he stopped his search and I gave a mental sigh of relief. How ironic that Winsome had missed the very place he used to conceal weapons himself.

He led me through the maze of boxes stacked floor to ceiling. The place felt different to how it had been when it was empty. Somehow the boxes made the place seem even more isolated and threatening. The boxes would serve to deaden the sound of any screaming, I couldn't help thinking. We reached a clearing in the centre of the boxes and the first thing I saw was Ella's naked body hanging like a piece of meat. Her head rested on her chest as if she was unconscious. The sight made me gasp.

"You fucking bastards! What have you done to my daughter?" I yelled, anger flowing over me like a tsunami.

Leon was sitting on a lone crate facing Ella. "You took your time getting here," he sneered. "Wake up Ella darling, Daddy's come to save you."

With that Leon moved faster than I'd ever seen and threw a bucket of water over Ella. She screamed and her body jerked on the rope as the shock of the cold liquid drenched her head and then ran in rivulets down her naked body. She saw me standing there helpless and begged, "Daddy, help me please!"

I had to fight down an urge to just pull out the gun nestling in the small of my back and start firing, but Leon, Mike and Winsome were standing well apart from each other and the chances of me actually hitting any of them, having never fired a gun before were pretty slim. Besides, they almost certainly had guns too and might start firing back. I had to stay cool and not panic if I was going to get both of us out alive. My plan was to delay things as long as possible in the hope that help would arrive in the shape of DJ Bruno Cannard whom I hoped was still listening in on the other end of my phone.

"You don't need to harm Ella. You've got me now so why don't you just let her go? She's never done anything to harm you," I said.

Leon appeared to consider this then he turned malevolently to me and said, "That's true, she's never done a thing to me but she's seen me now and, after what I'm going to do to a traitorous prick like you, I can't afford to leave any witnesses."

Saying that, he produced a baseball bat from beside the crate and began smacking it into his palm. "You've seen what we can do with this, haven't you. What part of your precious little girl shall we break first? Shall we start at the feet?"

Leon stood up and took a step toward Ella who stared at me in open eyed terror.

"For God's sake, Leon, you have a daughter yourself who's a similar age. Please think about what you're doing – let her go and I'll make her promise never to say a word about this," I pleaded.

Leon sat back down. I was aware of the seconds ticking by, knowing that every one was buying my rescuers a fraction more time.

The silence inside the warehouse was ominous as Leon kept me waiting for an answer. Eventually, he said, "My daughter doesn't do a bloody thing I tell her to do. So why should I believe yours will keep any promises she makes to you?"

"Because she'll know what you're capable of and that you'll hunt her down and kill her if she talks; she's not stupid! Please Leon, show some mercy."

"Are you saying my daughter's more stupid than yours?" Leon demanded, eyes blazing at me.

"You know that's not what I meant at all."

"Do I?"

Leon was just goading me now and I chose to say nothing.

Leon sat on the crate just staring at me, silently challenging me. I didn't rise to his bait so he said, "You're right, of course, I do have a daughter Ella's age and I would hate her to be in such a frightening predicament."

Leon stopped talking and looked from me to Ella and back again. Once again he let the silence build. I searched his face for signs that he might be relenting but all I saw were his cruel, fathomless eyes staring back at me.

Ella was the first to break the silence, "Please let me go,

I promise I won't say anything about you."

Leon pointed a finger and said, "Shut the fuck up bitch, or I'll tape your mouth shut again."

Ella looked as though an invisible hand had slapped her. Her shaking body sent shudders up the rope while a solitary tear trickled slowly down her cheek.

"You know," Leon said, "you're right. I am a father and, one father to another, I know how distressing it must be for you seeing your daughter trussed up like this. But do you know something, Martin? I want to see you suffer because of your disloyalty. I can't afford to have a grass in my organisation and when I find one I make them suffer as much as is humanly possible before they die. Your death will be an example to anyone else who might choose to talk about my affairs to the cops."

He paused glancing briefly at Mike and Winsome to be sure they were paying attention.

"Which is why, before I smash your daughter to bits in front of your eyes, I've decided, because of your pathetic pleading, to make her suffer a little more indignity by allowing my boys here to have some fun with her first."

Then he turned to Winsome and said, "Been a while since you've shagged anything this young, I'll bet. I hope you've got some protection though because there's no telling how many randy students have been through this little tart ahead of you!"

Leon laughed at his own joke. Meanwhile Winsome's hand went to loosen his belt buckle.

"That's enough!" I yelled tugging the gun out from my waistband and pointing it at Leon's head.

Everything froze as if suspended in a moment of time.

"Well, well, well," Leon sneered, not looking the least bit fazed by the gun as it shook in my hand. "I thought I asked you to frisk him, Winsome."

"I did boss," Winsome replied.

"Not well enough obviously!"

Winsome grunted.

235

The situation was far from ideal. My three opponents were spread out making it almost impossible to keep all of them in my field of vision without turning my head from side to side. Had Mike already taken a step closer to me? I couldn't be sure.

"The first thing you can do is drop your guns on the floor and kick them over to me."

"What makes you think we're tooled up, Marty?" asked Winsome.

"Because I know you too bloody well!"

Both Winsome and Mike looked at Leon who gave the tiniest nod of his head. They reached behind them.

"Ah, ah, left handed and very slowly please," I said.

They did exactly as they were told, kicking the guns well away from themselves.

"You too, Leon."

He stared coolly at me. "You must know I never carry guns, Martin. Why would I when I have these two to shoot for me?"

I don't know why but I believed him.

"Get her down, from there," I demanded, in a voice as shaky as my gun hand.

"Or what Martin?" Leon replied. "Are you going to shoot all three of us?"

"Just do as I say," I said. This time I caught Mike from the corner of my eye taking another step toward me and spun to face him. "Don't take another step, or else!"

Mike stood still and raised his hands in submission.

Leon said, "OK, Martin, easy now, we don't want that thing going off by accident do we? Are you sure you've knocked the safety catch off?"

I couldn't stop myself glancing down at the catch on the gun. Winsome took the opportunity to move a step closer. "If either of you move another step, I will shoot," I said. "Don't make me do it!"

Both men were now just a few feet away on either side of me.

I was distracted by the whirring sound of the crane being lowered. Leon had the operating console in his hands and was busy lowering Ella to the ground.

"OK, Martin, you can have your little girl back. No one needs to get hurt, you're the man with the gun and that makes you *the* man right now. You win!"

Leon was capitulating far too easily and I glanced suspiciously to my left, Winsome hadn't moved from the spot but something in his expression made me turn back. But I was too late! Mike had crept up on my other flank and I felt a hard blow on my wrist. The gun fired making a deafening sound and a piece of wood splintered harmlessly from a nearby crate. The blow, coupled with the recoil was enough to loosen the gun from my grip and send it clattering across the concrete floor. I took a step to try and retrieve it but Mike had a hold of my arm. I spun to try and free myself but in the intervening seconds Winsome had closed the gap and now had a strong grip on my other arm. Unlike both these men, I was no fighter. Mike landed a vicious uppercut into my solar plexus that took the wind right out of me and had the two men not hung onto my arms I would surely have buckled to the floor.

In the meantime, Leon had raised the crane back up so Ella's feet were once again swinging in the air. He picked up the gun while Mike and Winsome held me firmly upright between them.

Leon walked slowly towards us, looking thoughtfully at the gun. "I've killed with this gun before," he said. "You told me you'd got rid of it." He sighed, and looked to the ceiling. "You just can't get reliable staff.

"And now it's like déjà vu, I'm going to have to kill with it and dispose of it all over again. But don't worry, I have a beautiful garden ready to bury you and your daughter where you'll be together for eternity. I'm sure you can both take some comfort from that."

He stopped in front of me pointing the gun at my head. I could smell the cordite and feel the warmth of the barrel on my face. Another kind of warmth spread from my loins as my bladder emptied and I hung my head in shame; I'd failed Ella, my beautiful daughter. I couldn't bring myself to look at her one last time and instead shut my eyes tightly and clenched my teeth so hard my jaw ached as I braced myself for what was coming.

There was a loud bang followed almost immediately by another, not one but two shots fired in quick succession. I felt warm drops of liquid splatter my face, I heard Ella's piercing scream. Winsome's grip on my left arm slackened and I felt myself crashing to the floor. Mike let go of my right arm. There was shouting all around me. I couldn't understand why I could feel no pain. I was lying on something soft and uncomfortable. I knew the pain must come and waited for it to wash over me. Someone seemed to be yelling at me but I couldn't take in what they were saying. The warm liquid that had splashed onto my face ran down over my top lip. I tasted blood. Was I still alive? I felt so confused. Slowly I opened my eyes. Leon was lying underneath me and his face looked like it had been shredded. A pool of blood was spreading slowly beneath his head. Lying next to Leon, Winsome was staring up at me through dead glassy eyes, his chest was leaking blood all over his white shirt. A man wearing a black flak jacket, helmet and goggles had a gun trained upon Mike who was standing very still with his hands placed on his head. Other similarly clad men seemed to be everywhere. Two were helping Ella down off the hoist and another two came towards me.

One of the men said, "It's alright now, sir. You're safe. It's all over."

I sat up; dazed, bewildered. I wiped my face and looked down at a blood-smeared hand. I felt light-headed. Two officers helped me to my feet.

"Come with us, sir. Let's get you and your daughter out of here and cleaned up."

I looked over towards Ella. They'd put a blanket

around her shoulders and she was being guided gently towards the exit. I allowed myself to be led quietly away by the two men, one each side of me, propping me up on shaky legs.

CHAPTER THIRTY-TWO

After an interminable wait, I found myself back in the interview room sitting across from DI Bruno Cannard and another officer. Sitting next to me was a duty solicitor whose name I'd been told and instantly forgotten. I still hadn't been allowed to talk to Ella and felt frustrated. The formalities had been gone through and the recorders were running.

Cannard took me carefully through everything that had happened leading up to the events in the warehouse and what then transpired. Before the formal part of the interview began, Cannard had reassured me that Ella was alright and being well looked after. She too was giving her statement of events and as soon as both statements were completed we would be briefly reunited. We'd been kept separate so that we couldn't collude on our statements, Cannard had explained. I felt we were being treated like criminals and said so, but soon cooled down when Cannard reminded me I *was* a criminal, albeit one who was now cooperating with the police.

It took several hours, with only occasional stops for comfort breaks and regular refills of strong black coffee. The interview ended with Cannard formally arresting me but explaining that my part in exposing the criminal activities of Leon Spencer would be taken into account by the judge. Then he leaned forward to switch off the tapes and asked me to remain behind. My unnamed solicitor looked unhappy about any informality but reluctantly left the room while I remained firmly seated.

When it was just the two of us Cannard said, "We had to do that formal bit for the tapes, sorry, but I assure you, Martin, I will speak very highly of you in court. What you did for your daughter was foolish but heroic – you tried your best for Ella and believe me she knows it."

"I failed her though. If you hadn't come along we'd both be dead!" I felt tears well in my eyes and hung my head in shame.

Cannard took a hold of my wrists across the table. "Martin, look at me..."

I lifted my eyes and saw a look of genuine concern in Cannard's face.

Cannard continued. "Listen. You successfully delayed things and kept Ella unharmed until we were able to get into a position where we could act without endangering you or the lives of our officers. Leaving your phone switched on and then concealing it like that was a stroke of genius."

"What I don't quite understand is why they had to shoot Winsome?" I said.

"We didn't. And we wouldn't have shot Leon either if we hadn't thought your life was in immediate peril," Cannard explained. "Our marksman had to make a split-second decision and when he saw Leon's finger tightening on the trigger he felt he had to take the shot to save your life. Actually he left it a little late and when Leon was hit the gun in his hand went off and it was only the force of the impact that turned his gun hand towards Winsome. One man's good fortune is another's bad luck, as they say."

I swallowed as I realised just how close I'd come to death. I felt a mixture of feelings: guilt that I'd indirectly caused the death of two men and relief in the certain knowledge that Leon would not be seeking some kind of revenge on me from behind prison bars.

I was allowed an all too brief meeting with Ella where we held each other's hands. I began to apologise but Cannard had proved right and Ella wouldn't hear of it. In her eyes her father was a hero who had saved her life. I felt undeserving, having been the one who had placed her in danger in the first place but I didn't go there. No doubt my wife, Katrina would point that out to Ella sooner or later. She was apparently waiting downstairs right this minute to take her home.

*

I was taken before a magistrate who placed me on remand to await further proceedings. A couple of days later Beth visited me.

I felt grateful to her for coming.

Towards the end of her time she said, "I'll wait for you, Martin, if you want me to and whenever they let you out there'll be a job for you in the cafe too, if you want it."

I was stumped for words. Once again I could feel tears welling in my eyes and felt pathetic.

"Well?" she said. "If you want me to wait, that is!"

I felt almost too choked to speak. Eventually, I managed to say in a hoarse whisper, "I love you, Beth."

She leaned across the table and kissed my lips, then said, "Just hold onto that feeling."

THE END

ACKNOWLEDGMENTS

First and foremost I'd like to thank you, the reader, for reaching the end of the book and I sincerely hope you found it entertaining. If you could spare a little more of your time to write a brief online review it would be much appreciated as we indie-authors rely on reviews to help us get noticed.

I would also like to thank writer and friend Lesley Horton, former Chair of the Crime Writers Association, for her inspiration and encouragement; my many other writing friends at Cardiff Writers' Circle; The Tiny Writers' Group and CRAG for their comments on the early drafts; Lucy Ridout for her helpful and professional structural edit; Diana and Geoff for proof reading and suggestions for improvements; David Abbott for editing this 2nd edition; Chris for coming up with a better title than 'White Van Man'; Siobhan and Jon for their help with cover ideas and my mother Barbara Drake who, thanks to a misspelled surname on a store card, gave me the pen-name Darke.

ABOUT THE AUTHOR

Robert Darke was born and raised in Cardiff but then moved around the UK with his job in HM Customs and Excise before eventually returning to settle back in his home town. He left Customs to provide IT Security and Audit services for several major organisations in the private and public sectors. In 2013 he took early retirement from his job as Head of Corporate Communication for a large government agency to allow more time to concentrate on his writing.

He is also a keen photographer, hospital radio presenter and proud new member of the Harley-Davidson Owners Group (HOG) Great Western Chapter.

For more information please visit:
www.robertdarke.com
www.facebook.com/robertdarkewriter
www.twitter.com/robertdarke
www.robdarke.wordpress.com

33367804R00146

Printed in Great Britain
by Amazon